LEADING LINES

A PIPPA GREENE NOVEL

Chantel Guertin

ECW Press

Published by ECW Press
665 Gerrard Street East
Toronto, ON M4M 1Y2
416-694-3348 / info@ecwpress.com

Library and Archives Canada
Cataloguing in Publication

Guertin, Chantel, 1976–, author
Leading lines : a Pippa Greene novel /
Chantel Guertin.

Issued in print and electronic formats.
ISBN 978-1-77041-232-3 (pbk)
978-1-77090-757-7 (PDF)
978-1-77090-758-4 (ePub)

Editor for the press: Crissy Calhoun
Cover images: © Melina Souza
(www.melinasouza.com)
Author photo: Steven Khan

The publication of *Leading Lines* has been generously supported by the Canada Council for the Arts which last year invested $157 million to bring the arts to Canadians throughout the country, and by the Ontario Arts Council (OAC), an agency of the Government of Ontario, which last year funded 1,793 individual artists and 1,076 organizations in 232 communities across Ontario, for a total of $52.1 million. We also acknowledge the financial support of the Government of Canada through the Canada Book Fund for our publishing activities, and the contribution of the Government of Ontario through the Ontario Book Publishing Tax Credit and the Ontario Media Development Corporation.

PRINTED AND BOUND IN CANADA BY FRIESENS   5 4 3 2 1

*For Chris, Myron, Penny
and Fitz—my world*

THE RULE OF THIRDS

"The story flows nicely, has believable characters and will appeal to readers looking for a realistic tale with a bit of romance."
—*School Library Journal*

"If you like stories about trying to find yourself while dealing with the ultimate grief of losing a parent, like Eileen Cool's *Unraveling Isobel*, then you won't be able to put this one down." —*Faze Magazine*

"Chantel Guertin has created a lovable character with Pippa Greene, and a lovable book with *The Rule of Thirds*." —Alice Kuipers, author of *40 Things I Want to Tell You*

"Part romance, part tearjerker, part friendship story—this terrific read will capture your heart." —Sarah Mlynowski, author of *Ten Things We Did (and Probably Shouldn't Have)*

"Chantel Guertin creates a realistic, poignant story about loss, love, friendship and finding light in darkness. *The Rule of Thirds* is a fresh, endearing novel that will capture your heart, expose a smile and stay in your memory like a favorite family photo."
—Laura Bowers, author of *Beauty Shop for Rent* and *Just Flirt*

"A major plot twist doesn't involve friend drama and has little to do with boys, which is hard to find in YA. Also rare is how realistically Pippa is drawn . . . she's presented as capable, thoughtful and intellectual without being clichéd." —*Quill & Quire*

"Guertin's voice is impeccable, believably channeling a 16-year-old girl who must learn the uncomfortable reality that life is not a fairytale, and not all stories end happily ever after. The resulting novel is surprisingly upbeat as Pippa copes with normal life marching on—often with hilarious results." —National Reading Campaign

"*The Rule of Thirds* ventures beyond the mundane comforts of the average teenage problem novel, and instead explores deeper issues using a creative plot and a flowing narrative, helping to solidify this novel as a well-rounded and engaging option for readers. Recommended." —*CM: Canadian Review of Materials*

"You'll fall in love with this genuine young heroine as she experiences the ups and downs of being a teen while dealing with the loss of her dad."
—*Best Health*

DEPTH OF FIELD

"Amusingly honest . . . Frothy yet engaging romance with a snapshot of the photography world to add color." —*Kirkus Reviews*

"With an upbeat tone, clever dialogue and an artsy point of view, *Depth of Field* is one relatable teenage girl's contemporary coming-of-age journey." —*School Library Journal*

"Tight plotting, vivid characters and an underlying thread of photography know-how make *Depth of Field* a smart and stylish read." —*National Reading Campaign*

"Guertin truly inhabits the world of a talented 16-year-old who, in spite of self-doubt, faces the world head-on. And if the story is one that has been told many times, many ways, Guertin's approach to it is creative and new." —*CM: Canadian Review of Materials*

"It's nice to see a heroine who has both feet on the ground. She's genuine: with one foot she steps out to the future; the other clawing her back as she deals with the personal loss. Pippa is not the clichéd heroine you'd expect in a YA novel." —*Sukasa Reads*

"Just as emotional of a read as the last book . . . sweet and touching." —*Words of Mystery*

"Anyone who is looking for some quick and fun reads but still wants to find a reason to get invested in a story and a character's journey needs to look no further than Guertin's Pippa Greene series." —*Read My Breath Away*

"If you enjoy realistic YA fiction with an authentic voice, I'd recommend this series." —*Ramblings of a Daydreamer*

"Pippa is an appealing heroine and this will find readers." —*VOYA*

CHAPTER 1

"Pippa Greene, please report to the office. Pippa Greene, to the office, please."

Less than five minutes into the first day back after winter break and my name's called over the PA system. I stand, and so does the hair on my arms. In my time at Spalding High, I've only been called to the office twice. There's a bunch of oohs around the room.

"The rules! You're breaking the rules!" Dace quotes. We had to read *Lord of the Flies* over the break for English Lit and Dace actually read it. Then we watched the movie. That Balthazar Getty may be ancient now, but he was super cute in the movie.

"Hurry back. You don't want to miss all the fun," Mr. Alderman says a little overzealously. Mr. Alderman is new. All I know about him is that he's filling in for Mrs. Murphy, who was my homeroom and English

Lit teacher, while she's on mat leave. And now, all he knows about me is that I got called down to the office within minutes of a new term. Not exactly the impression I was going for. I grab my white ski jacket off the back of my chair—the trek between the portable and the school is too frosty without it—and pull it on. My heart picks up speed as I yank open the door to the portable, a gust of cold air hitting me in the face. I pull my hood over my head and hurry down the three steps to the snow-covered pavement to the back door of the school, burying my chin beneath the stand-up collar.

The main office is bustling with students bringing down attendance forms and latecomers signing in. And there's Ben Baxter, standing in front of a tall gray filing cabinet, holding a colorful stack of file folders. He smiles when he sees me. He got a haircut over the break: it's shorter on the sides and back and a bit longer on top. He's wearing a navy mock-neck sweater, making his blue eyes pop. My stomach flip-flops.

"In trouble already?" he teases.

I give him a look. "I'm sure it's nothing." My face heats up and I look away. Mrs. Pinkrose is shuffling papers at the front desk. She's the main office admin lady, the one who called me down to the office. "I probably forgot a mitten or something over the break."

"Yeah, I heard Forsythe has a New Year's resolution to run a very personal lost and found system." He grins.

I roll my eyes, then shuffle toward the row of

green vinyl chairs that line the glass windows of the office. Ben comes over and sits beside me, placing the folders on his lap.

"Maybe you're getting an award for putting up with me in New York." He leans over, knocking my shoulder with his.

I glance his way, quickly, then focus on the large white clock on the wall. "What are you doing here, anyway?" I ask him, to change the subject.

"Detention," he says, as though I should know. "No spares for the wicked."

I raise my eyebrows.

"What?"

"You're still doing detention for stealing everyone's stuff?"

"Hey, you were the number one casualty. If you think it's been too long, maybe you could put in a good word when you're in there." He raises his eyebrows.

"Not likely." I smirk at him, so he knows there's no hard feelings. But detention? He totally earned it. "How much longer do you have?"

"Rest of the year. Every day. First period."

"So there really *is* justice in the world."

"Can we move on?" He tosses the folders on the table at the end of the row of chairs. I look up to see if Mrs. Pinkrose is taking any of this in, but she's oblivious. "So how was your break?" We haven't seen each other since we got back from our two weeks in New York before the Christmas break. Which was kind of an intense two weeks, especially since at the end of it he wasn't going to finish his year at Spalding, but I asked him to come back. And he did.

"Great, fine," I say, wiping my palms on my jeans. How much longer am I going to have to wait out here?

"What you'd do?"

"Christmas family stuff." I press my lips together. "And um, just hung out with Dylan."

"Huh." He nods. His phone buzzes and he pulls it out. I look away but a second later, he nudges me. "Remember this?" On his phone is a familiar photo of two round shapes.

On the bus ride home from New York, Ben and I sat together, but it was awkward, at least to start. I don't know what Ben was thinking, but I was all over the place. Which was making me act weird. So our conversation was stilted and confusing. Until Ben pointed out the two guys in front of us. Their heads were *exactly* the same. Shaved in that way that men do when they're prematurely balding, because you could see stubble in some spots and not in others. Ben thought it was odd, that they were friends with the same male-pattern baldness, until I told Ben about how girls get their periods at the same time if they hang out all the time and he told me that was TMI, though he actually looked fascinated with this fact, and it sort of broke the ice. And then we started really analyzing the two guys, trying to figure out their story, but whispering so they wouldn't overhear us. Ben got up to go to the front of the bus, as though he were asking the driver a question, and on his way back he snapped a pic of the pair on his phone, then slid back into the seat beside me and showed me the craziest thing of all. They were man-twins. Like, they had to be our moms' age and dressed exactly the same: same jeans, same golf shirt—one in red, the other in blue. Same rectangular rimless glasses. Ben wondered if their underwear matched too.

After the novelty of the man-twins wore off, Ben suggested we watch a movie on his iPad. I figured he'd have nothing outside the Marvel universe and was about to say no and just sleep, but he suggested *Before Sunrise*.

The movie was about this guy and girl—Jesse and Céline—who meet on a train from Budapest and end up sitting together and talking about random stuff. They get off the train in Vienna and have this set of adventures overnight and there's totally chemistry between the two of them. In that way it wasn't *really* like Ben and me on the bus, because I was still really thinking about how much I missed Dylan and wanting to see him, but the beginning of the movie was pretty oddly similar to us, and I joked that this was an Art Imitating Life moment, and Ben sort of nodded and I realized he must've known that's what the movie was about and that's why he picked it and I felt sort of silly and naïve, but he didn't say so.

After the movie ended we sat in that sleepy silence, tired but also sort of feeling like we were having an adventure ourselves—even though we were just sitting on a bus. At least, that's how I was feeling. Maybe it was that it was the conclusion of a two-week adventure, and we'd been on it—or through it—together, which was the last thing I'd ever expected. I didn't want to fall asleep because I knew if I did, I'd wake up groggy in Spalding and it would all be over. And even though I didn't know what it meant, I didn't *want* this part with Ben to be over.

As the sleepiness faded, Ben brought up the subject of his dad, who was the whole reason he'd gone to New York. And then he asked what happened with David, my Tisch mentor, who turned out to be my dad. Which was already just this huge shock to digest, but then on the final night I caught David making out with Savida, one of the other Tisch campers, which completely messed with my already messy emotions.

Once we finally got past all the father drama, we settled into just talking. About music, about books, about Ben's friends back in Cheektowaga, about how much we'd miss Ramona and the rest of the Tisch crew, and about life and everything else.

And then the bus pulled into the depot in Spalding, and it was over. I got off first, and Ben followed me and we picked up our bags from beside the bus, and then Ben carried mine over to the curb. He looked at me and did this funny riff on *Before Sunrise*, where they plan to meet at the same spot in six months: "See you in two weeks?" he said. "Right here." And I laughed, and then he leaned in and then we had this hug that lasted just a bit longer than necessary. Like, totally innocent but also . . . charged.

"Hey, where's that from?" Ben says now. I follow his gaze, down to the pocket of my ski jacket where

I still have a lift ticket looped through my zipper pull.

"Oh, Holiday Valley. In Ellicottville?"

"You went skiing?"

"Yeah. Dace's mom and stepdad have a condo there. Dace invited Dylan and me up."

Mrs. Pinkrose clears her throat and gives Ben a set of raised eyebrows. He stands and grabs his stack of folders.

"I didn't know you ski." He opens the filing cabinet, but is looking at me.

"I don't. It was my first time. I was pretty terrible." I pull one of my legs up under me and turn to face him.

"It takes a few tries to really get it." He closes one drawer, walks his fingers along the file tabs and slides the folder in.

"We only went overnight." There were adjoining rooms at the condo—so Dace and I shared and Dylan got his own room, and it was super easy to sneak over there in the middle of the night. And even though my three-month rule was basically up when we were there, we didn't do it, but we definitely made some progress. Let's just say we may have been at a ski resort, but we covered a lot of baseball bases. I don't know what taking off your long underwear under the covers possibly counts as—shortstop?! Third?

"You should join ski club," Ben says.

"We don't have a ski club," I point out.

"We do. Or we will, if my club request goes through."

"It's 9:15. You're already organizing a ski club?"

"There are benefits to having office-duty detention." He pops a file in place and opens another drawer. "It's 20 bucks a week, and you get the bus there and back and the lift ticket. We leave at 3 on Fridays and get back to the school parking lot at midnight." He files the final folder and shuts the top drawer of the cabinet, giving it two taps on top just as Principal Forsythe sticks his head out his door and calls my name.

I stand and hurry into his office.

"Don't look so worried," Forsythe says, closing the door as I sink into one of the two black fabric chairs in front of his desk. He makes his way to the swivel chair on the other side of his desk. His office looks like it got the 24-hour flu: papers are scattered over his desk and floor, there's an empty box upended in the corner, a pen by my feet, and his recycling bin is overflowing. His appearance is kind of the same—his white-and-gray striped shirt is wrinkled, the top button is MIA and his glasses are crooked.

Catching my expression, he says, "My new year's resolution is to get organized. But that old adage is true—before things can get better they must get worse. Just don't let Mrs. Pinkrose see the place. Anyway, let's get to it." He rubs his hands together, and I shrug out of my ski jacket since I'm starting to sweat.

"This year marks the 50th anniversary of Spalding High, if you can even believe it. Fifty years! I'd like to say I don't remember when the school opened, but I was in first grade and it was a big deal in town. Anyway, point is, we're having an alumni reunion dance on Valentine's Day." He looks at me like I should know *why* he's telling me this. I nod encouragingly.

"What I'd like from you and the photo club is to coordinate some sort of photo display for the dance that celebrates our 50 years and our students."

"What did you have in mind?" I ask.

"No idea!" Principal Forsythe pushes his glasses up his nose. "I've got a ton of other details to work out. So I leave this in your capable hands. Talk to your fellow photographers and get back to me."

"OK, sounds great," I tell him.

"Excellent." He claps his hands together and ushers me out.

I head through the office to the hall; Ben follows me. "Everything good?"

I nod. "Oh, yeah, just something for photo club."

"Something cool?"

"I'll tell everyone at the meeting. Today after school—new time, same second-rate room. I should get back to class."

"Ski club. Think about it, Pippa Greene!" he says dramatically.

"Can't. Fridays are date night."

He shakes his head. "How are you going to get better at skiing sitting on a couch watching movies?"

I laugh, roll my eyes and then turn and head off down the hall. "Later, Ben Baxter."

CHAPTER 2

I wait until we're wrapping up photo club that afternoon to mention the reunion dance project.

"Is this optional?" Jeffrey grumbles, looking up from his laptop.

"Well, I think Principal Forsythe thought it would be fun for us. An opportunity."

"Don't need it. Too much with my independent study." He closes his laptop and slips it into his backpack, then stands.

"Me too," says Arlan, getting up. "Sorry, Pippa." He pulls on his coat.

"I don't mind helping out," Gemma says.

I look around the room. Brooke shakes her head. "Can't. I've got a heavy schedule this term." That's everyone. Except Ben.

"I'm in," he says, leaning back in his chair.

"OK, so . . . three of us?" I'm grateful that Gemma's in, because otherwise: no Ben buffer.

As everyone packs up, I check my phone again to see if Dylan's texted, but my screen's blank. I shove it in my back pocket and put my camera and laptop into my bag, then sling it across my body and grab my coat off the desk beside me. Maybe he's just waiting in the parking lot.

I make a beeline for the door so I don't have to walk out with Ben. I don't want Dylan to think we're all chummy or anything.

"Pip, wait up," Gemma calls, her tight black curls bouncing as she rushes to catch up. I pause as she falls into step with me. "This'll be fun," she says.

"We just have to come up with an idea," I say.

"You'll think of something, you always do." She laughs as we push through the front doors. "Oh, there's Emma," she says and waves at her twin who's just pulling into the lot. "See you tomorrow."

"'Kay," I say, giving her a wave, then looking around the parking lot for Dylan's dad's car. He's not here. We didn't exactly text to confirm, but he's been picking me up after school ever since, well, ever since he became my boyfriend. I call, but it goes straight to voicemail. I hang up and slip my phone in my coat pocket then pull my camera out of my bag. The afternoon sun is reflecting in the icicles hanging from the gutters, and I tilt my head back, holding my camera steady to capture the light reflection—this week's photo club theme.

"Need a ride?" a familiar voice says behind me, but

I don't move. I pull the camera away from my face and check the screen. Not enough zoom. I sigh and turn around. Ben's throwing his book bag over his shoulder. I scan the parking lot for Dylan's car again.

"Waiting for a better offer?" he teases.

"Ha ha. Dylan's supposed to pick me up. I should probably just wait." I check my phone for the millionth time but there's only the pic of Dylan and me skating. I feel nostalgic for winter break, when Dylan and I hung out every day, even though it just ended yesterday. Dylan planned that romantic skating date for us: he'd read online about this continuous path you could skate on. We packed a backpack with snacks and hot chocolate and made the hour drive. There was a parking lot at the start of the path where we left the car and bundled up—hats, mitts, scarves and extra pairs of socks—then headed out on the route. We planned to make it as far as our toes could last the cold, stop for a hot chocolate and snack break, then skate back. We figured it would take hours. At first we could only see a small section of the path in front of us. We were holding hands and chatting, when, just two minutes later, we rounded some reeds and trees and realized we were back at the start of the trail again. The rink was a figure eight. We looked at each other and started laughing—and couldn't stop. For some reason we thought it was the funniest thing. That's when we took the pic. We did another couple loops, then got back in the car and caught an early matinee movie instead. It was one of our best dates yet.

Of course, in some ways, this Christmas was the worst one yet—Mom and my first Christmas without Dad, and being upset with Mom about the whole David secret—but being with Dylan made it one of my favorites. Which felt wrong, but I guess that's how things go. Sometimes bad things open your eyes to how good other things can be.

I shove my phone in my pocket and pull up the collar on my coat as a gust of wind whips by.

"All right, see you tomorrow," Ben calls, already a few steps into the parking lot.

"Wait!" I say, hurrying to catch up. "I'm too cold to wait any longer."

He clicks the key fob. The lights on his black BMW SUV flash twice.

I scan the street leading into the lot once more before climbing in, then slink down in the leather seat as I put on my seatbelt, not crazy about people seeing us together. If Ben notices, he doesn't say anything.

"Home?"

Home. "Actually, could you drive me to Dace's?" I say, texting Dace to see if it's OK if I come over. The last thing I want to do is go home.

"Trouble in Greeneland?"

I didn't realize I had said that last bit out loud. I blush. "Oh, no. Just . . . yeah."

"Your mom?" He lowers the volume on the radio.

"Yeah."

"You told her you found out about David?" Ben and I had talked a lot on the bus ride home about whether or not I should tell Mom that I know. He made a pretty convincing case for being honest, especially since I was so upset with her for keeping such a big secret. Hypocrisy, and all that.

I fiddle with the door lock. "You were right. I couldn't *not* tell her, and I guess I wanted to hear what she had to say. But what *could* she say? And now it's *out there*, but I'm so angry with her. And I can't hide it."

"It was a huge secret that she kept, for sure," Ben says. "Did she explain why she and your dad decided not to tell you that David was your birth father?"

"Just that my dad wanted to be my father. David didn't. Simple. Which I knew. I guess I wanted to hear something else. Something more. Something that made it all feel less . . . random. Something to make it all right."

"Hmm. That sucks." We're stopped at a red light. An army of dogs yank on their leashes, practically dragging a girl with dreadlocks and harem pants across the intersection.

"Yeah, it does. And now she wants me to tell David I know. Which, if you think about it, makes no sense. She didn't tell me because she didn't want David in my life, and now she does? And I don't." I sigh, getting a flash of David making out with Savida at the end-of-Tisch-camp party. The light turns green and we start to move.

"Maybe she's feeling guilty. Maybe now, since your dad is gone and David being part of your life can't make him feel bad, maybe . . . I dunno maybe she's just trying to do the right thing? Whatever that is?"

He's probably right about my mom, but I don't

feel like cutting her any slack at the moment. "Turn here," I say, pointing toward Everleigh Road. He turns. We're both quiet until a few minutes later when we pull into Dace's driveway.

"I didn't even ask you about your mom. How are things going?"

He shrugs. "Fine, fine. Another time." He puts the car in park. The seatbelt whirrs as it retreats into its holster and I grab my bag from where I'd tossed it on the floor.

"Well, thanks for the ride."

"Anytime."

I get out and head for the front door as he reverses down the driveway.

Dace is waiting with the door open, wearing a floppy black wool hat over her long blonde hair and woolly-mammoth-like furry pull-on slippers. She raises her eyebrows as Ben's car disappears down the street.

"What?" I say defensively, as she pulls me inside and quickly closes the door. "It's no big deal. Dylan didn't show, and I needed a ride." I kick off my snowy boots and then straighten them on the mat by the door. She pulls off my coat and hangs it on one of the hooks on the wall.

"And Ben just happened to be hanging around?" She squeezes past me, and I follow her down the hall.

"Photo club, remember?"

She lumbers up the dark wood stairs in her ridiculous slippers, her long legs taking the steps two at a time. "Dylan needs to step up his game, because Ben is homing back in."

I follow her up to her room. "I completely set Ben straight. I've mentioned Dylan and our wonderful Christmas break about a zillion times. He *gets* it. We're just friends."

"No need to get so defensive," Dace says, pulling on the sleeves of her gray cable-knit sweater and plopping down at her desk. "So you ready to accessorize our school stuff? My mom said I can spend $100, but we'll just split it two ways." Dace has this idea that if she gets really cute binders and pens, she'll actually take pride in doing her homework and getting good grades this term. At first I was very impressed with her New Year's resolution. I thought it was a result of her volunteer placement last term with the after-school homework club and I was going on and on about how the volunteer placements really *were* so good in the end (I got a boyfriend! Dace started caring about homework!), until she revealed her mom and stepdad said if she gets straight As this term they'll buy her a car in June.

Dace doesn't much like her stepfather, but she seems to be coming around, after a winter break at his chalet and now this bribe.

"I made a Pinterest board for inspiration," she says, flipping open her laptop.

"Of school accessories?"

She looks at me over her shoulder, raising her eyebrows. "Oh, I didn't think of that. No, of driving accessories. These Coach gloves, this cute hat from Anthropologie, that sort of thing." She leans out of the way so I can see. "But a board of stationery essentials is a great idea. And more suited to the task at hand." She starts a new board. "Ooh, I've got the best name for it." She types "The Write Stuff" and hits return. "Sometimes I'm brilliant."

I lie back on her bed and stare up at the ceiling, which is decked out in strings of white lights and wispy netting.

My phone rings. I sit up and grab it from the end of the bed. Dylan.

"Hey," I say, my heart thumping.

"Hey yourself. What's up? You called. Seven times." There's a teasing tone in his voice, but still I blush, feeling stupid and glad he can't see me.

"I just thought you were going to pick me up after school?" I say. "It was really cold out. Maybe the windchill went to my head."

"Oh crap. Did we say that?"

"No, I just . . . assumed." I pull my knees up to my chin and hug them with my free arm.

"I wasn't really thinking that you were back at school, I guess. And I just got up—I didn't realize it was already after 4."

"Oh," I say, not able to hide my surprise. "Did you sleep all day?"

"Luxury of the gap year," he jokes. I laugh, but I get a flash of worry: what does he do all day while I'm at school? "You home now?"

"No, I went to Dace's." I bite my bottom lip.

"You walked all the way there? I thought you said it was freezing out."

"No, uh . . . Gemma gave me a ride after photo club." Dace is making a "You're such a liar" face at me, but I bug my eyes out at her in response. No way am I telling him Ben Baxter drove me, out of the blue and over the phone.

"Cool. Well, call me later, kay?"

"OK."

"Love you, girl."

"Me too."

I flop back down on the bed as I hang up.

"When did Gemma get her black Bimmer?" Dace teases.

"I don't want him to be jealous for no reason."

"Well, if there's no reason, then you shouldn't worry, right? And lying . . ." She makes an "eek" face. "Plus Ben's in photo club, and you guys are no longer mortal enemies. This may not be a one-time thing."

"I know it's just . . ." I roll over to my side and face her.

"You got a bad case of the guilts." She twists around so she's facing me too, straddling her chair backwards, her arms slung over the back.

"*Yes.* I keep thinking if Dylan started hanging out with an ex-girlfriend, I'd be jealous. Even if he said there was nothing to be jealous about."

"Aaand Dylan doesn't know the whole story. Or even half the story."

"Exactly. Unless I tell him how much time Ben and I spent together in New York, and the whole Ben and his dad thing and how we bonded over that, it's weird that I'm suddenly *not* anti-Ben. And if I do tell him, it's weird that I haven't already told him. It's just simpler if the Ben thing doesn't come up."

Dace pops off her chair. "You want a Coke?"

"Yes. No. I think caffeine will make me crazier."

She nods. "You know the problem isn't caffeine, right? It's two little words."

I make a face. "I never should've told you!" What Dace is talking about, what I know she means, is the two words I said to Ben in New York.

Dace puts her hand on her heart and reaches out to me, OTT-acting-style: "Don't go!"

I throw a pillow at her, which she dodges, and we both laugh.

"Are you regretting it yet?"

I groan. "Yes. Though over the break it wasn't a problem. Out of sight and out of mind and all that. I just didn't reply to his texts. Now that we're back at school . . ."

"You can't pretend you didn't beg Ben Baxter to come back to Spalding with you."

"Yeah. And who *says* that? Who says 'Don't go' all dramatically?"

"I could totally see myself doing that. But you?" She shakes her head. "It's just not like you."

"Thanks for rubbing it in." I think back to that night, running to the subway to catch him before he left New York, to our trip back to Spalding and to today at school. "And really besides that . . . lapse of judgment, I haven't given him *any* reason to think that I'm into him. I have been very platonic all day. And ignored him for the whole break."

"Pippa," Dace says, sitting down on the end of the bed, where she keeps a fuzzy white faux-fur blanket, "he basically professed his love for you, and then you told him not to move away. So platonic signals are maybe too subtle. You're going to have to actually tell him you're not into him if you're not into him."

"Which I'm not."

She nods. "You know, it's OK if you are. It's kind of natural: he's hot, he's into you, you bonded in your parental distress, you were in magical Manhattan and Dylan was miles away. We all want to be loved, and sometimes absence doesn't make the heart grow fonder, it just makes you feel sad and lonely."

"That's profound," I say.

"I told you, I'm really going to brush up on my smarts this term." She smiles. "All I'm saying is don't be so quick to discount your feelings. But at the same time, Ben's your friend and you have to let him know if romance is off the table."

My phone buzzes and I grab it. Dace gets up and leaves the room.

Ben: Join ski club!

Me: Sno-go

Ben: So punny. But seriously.

I toss my phone aside as Dace walks back into the room with two glasses of water and hands me one.

"Ben's bugging me to join ski club." I roll my eyes.

"Oh yeah, do it! I signed up today."

I stare at her, mouth open. "Are you kidding?"

She takes a sip of water and shakes her head, shrugging, then sits back down at her desk.

I text Ben again.

Me: U hijacked my BFF?

Ben: And the twins. Gemma & Emma. Not man-twins from bus. That would be weird.

"Tell him you're in," Dace calls over her shoulder.

"Fridays are my date night with Dylan."

She turns to face me. "Can't you change date night?"

"To what? Saturdays are *our* night," I say, batting my eyelashes at her.

She points a bright pink nail-polished finger at me. "Good point. Sleepover Saturdays are sacred."

"See? I've thought this through."

"Huh. Well, I'm gonna miss you." She focuses back in on her computer screen for a split second. "Ooh, we should definitely get these rainbow Sharpies."

I glance at the blank screen on my phone, then toss it back in my bag, thinking about how Emma and Gemma and Dace will be off snowboarding every Friday night with Ben. Sure, I didn't really think about what they were doing on Fridays the past few months when Dylan and I were having date night, but now, for some reason, I feel left out.

CHAPTER 3

At least a foot of snow has fallen by the time I leave Dace's. I take the route through the woods, where the wind has created drifts, like the peaks on a lemon meringue pie. My thoughts drift to Dylan and why things feel off. The break was pretty much perfect, even though it got off to a shaky start: my homecoming wasn't exactly like I'd envisioned. Dylan was supposed to be back in Spalding first, and before we'd parted I'd given him my arrival information. So I kind of thought he'd be there, waiting for me at the bus terminal, like in the movies, only sketchier, because the Spalding bus terminal hasn't been updated since the '80s, so the seats have ripped vinyl, with yellowed foam bursting out or restrained by duct tape. And the walls are dismal gray and have random stains and the floors are dirty and there are always people lying in the corners.

But he wasn't there. I decided the communication ban was officially over, so I texted him while Mom drove me home from the bus station, and then again before bed. He didn't reply and I assumed he wasn't back yet. On Sunday morning I put together the album of photos I'd made for him from New York and took it over to his house to wait for him to get home. (He gave me a key a while ago, so even if his parents weren't home, I wouldn't be stuck on the porch in the snow.) But when I got there, he answered the door and while he seemed happy to see me, he didn't apologize for being in the same area code and not letting me know.

My irritation subsided pretty quickly though, because just the sight of him tends to make me forget my train of thought on typical days, and after not having seen him in more than two weeks, it's like he got even better looking. His caramel-colored hair, which lightens in the summer seemed darker than ever, making his green eyes even more intense. He hadn't shaved in a few days, so his dimple was hidden until he grinned, and then it was game over. And then he pulled me into the kind of kiss that caused every cliché in the best possible way: I got weak in the knees, got butterflies in my stomach and felt lightheaded all at once. If I weren't kissing, I would've sworn I was having a panic attack. (Turns out, a panic attack feels strangely similar to being head over heels in love.) We went straight to his room and nestled together on the bed for a bit. Later, he went to the closet and took out a bag of souvenirs for me: a t-shirt of one of the opening bands he liked and a handful of used guitar picks (not that I've ever played guitar). He had all these stories to go with each pick, and he relayed them with relish. And then I gave him his photo album. It was totally old school, plastic sleeves and everything, and held my favorite shots from New York—stuff that reminded me of him when I was there. This huge window display of Twizzlers in Times Square, the bright sign on the entrance to Dylan's Candy Bar at 60th and 3rd, a car with a license plate that said *DYLAN* and a bunch of other random stuff.

And he really listened as I told him about each photo, but about halfway through the album, I realized it felt like, *Hey, here's an album of my life over the last two weeks that has almost nothing to do with you.* And I could see that his eyes were sort of glazing over, and I got it, because that was how I felt on guitar pick number five of seven, and I realized maybe we were more into the gifts we were giving each other than the ones we got, if that makes any sense. So then I sped through the rest of the photos, quickly mentioning Ramona and some of the other Tisch campers and some of the highlights of my time away. He didn't seem to mind how I was rushing, which made me relieved that I caught his cues and didn't drag out the vacation-photo slideshow any longer, even if it also made me feel a little deflated.

Once I closed the album, I couldn't help but blurt out what had been bugging me for days.

"Why didn't you reply to my texts?" I fiddled with the edge of his comforter, pulling at a loose thread.

"What texts?" he asked. He stretched out, hands behind his head on his pillow.

"I texted you. Last Wednesday. And Thursday."

"You broke the ban?" He nudged me playfully in the side; I swatted his arm away.

"It was important."

He sat up and faced me. "What happened?"

"You really didn't get the texts?"

He shook his head and explained he'd gotten a new phone a few days into the tour. "I spilled beer all over mine on the third night. Maybe they came through between phones?" His casual mention of beer threw me (he wasn't drinking before he left, on the oncologist's recommendation). And even if he had missed those texts while he was away, surely he got the one I sent the previous day, but he made no mention of it. Instead, he pulled out his shiny new iPhone from the back pocket of his jeans. "Well, the ban's off now, right?" A second later my phone beeped.

Dylan: Boyfriend Alert!

I smiled and looked up at Dylan, trying to brush off my annoyance—how was he to know I'd had a major life crisis?—but he was engrossed in his phone, texting someone else and I wanted to ask who. Not that Dylan doesn't have his own life, but he doesn't really have a lot of friends that he kept in touch with after graduation. He didn't let anyone know he had cancer, so he lost touch with a lot of his guy friends who went away to college. Most people think he's on a BFL—a Break From Life, taking a year off between high school and college.

He leaned over to place his phone on the night-stand beside his bed and turned back to me, grabbing one of my hands and holding it between his. "So what was the crisis?"

So I told him. All about David. He listened to the whole sordid story and didn't try to do that guy thing where they solve the problem, he just listened, and then told me he was sorry he wasn't there for me when it was all going down.

I switched the topic of conversation over to him, and he told me all about his two weeks away, which couldn't have been more different than mine. How they hit a different town every day, a different venue every night. About how they tried to stop at all the diners from *Diners, Drive-Ins and Dives* along the route. How they stayed up until 4 in the morning and slept till 2 in the afternoon. How they played name that tune on the bus and poker in the hotel rooms.

I listened, but it was like watching a movie from the halfway point. You're not invested in the charac-ters, because you can't quite get them straight. And as he was telling me all of the stuff that happened to him, all I could think of was how much fun he had. How much fun he had without me. And so, instead of feeling happy for him, I felt glum and distant.

But then, we were tired of talking. And we snug-gled into each other. I pulled out the Sabres blanket he'd sent with me to New York, and we put on a movie, and then we ended up not really watching it, and I stopped worrying about our time apart and instead focused on our being back together.

• • •

"I made pancakes," Mom says when I come downstairs the next morning. She's hovering over her iPad at the kitchen counter, coffee mug in hand. I eye the table. In addition to the pile of pancakes, there's whipped cream and strawberries.

"I was feeling bad that I left you to fend for your own dinner last night. I can't seem to say no to the overtime shifts."

By the time I came home from Dace's, it was well after 8, and I'd eaten at her house without even calling to let Mom know. But I don't tell her that, because I already feel lousy for not having a part-time job while she's picking up any extra shifts she can get.

"I'm not hungry," I say, ignoring my grumbling stomach.

"Come on, Pippa. You can't keep punishing me."

"I'm not."

I turn and face her. She takes a sip of coffee. "Can you just sit?"

"Fine." I shuffle over to the table and put my apple down a little too forcefully.

She joins me. "Well, how was school yesterday? How were your classes?"

"Fine."

"Come on, tell me about the teachers. Anyone good?"

"New homeroom teacher."

"She's nice?"

"*He*. Yeah. Can I go?"

"Fine. But take a pancake with you?"

I grab one off the top of the pile and take a bite as I walk down the hall. I put on my boots, coat and hat, then sling my bag over my shoulder. I pause. "Really good pancake." Then I'm out the door.

CHAPTER 4

"Hey Pippa. Quick question," Ben says when he sees me coming out of last period later in the week. "Your mom works for a vet, right?"

"Yeah. At Furry Friendz."

"Is it a good place?"

"I guess? As far as vet clinics go. It's not a puppy mill or anything, if that's what you're asking."

"Can I get the details? My cat's wheezing and my mom's worried. And we don't have a vet in Spalding yet."

I pull out my phone and send him the contact for Mom at work. "I'll tell my mom. What's your cat's name?"

"Catniss."

"Funny. Kay, tell your mom to give Catniss's name on the phone." I stop at my locker and focus on the combination lock.

"You come up with an idea for the alumni event yet?" he asks.

I shake my head. "Nothing I'm excited about."

"Well, I've got something," he says.

"What is it?" I open my locker and toss my books in, then grab my camera and a notebook.

"Want to grab a coffee and discuss? I've got my car here."

"Can't. I've got *Hall Pass* in 10 minutes," I say, slinging my Rebel over my shoulder and shutting my locker.

"I'll walk you." He falls into step beside me as we head down the hall toward the photocopy room. "OK, so, what if we interview Spalding alumni and ask them their favorite memory of Spalding?"

"Like my Streeters column in the paper?" Finally, all that practice asking hard-nosed journalistic questions like "What's your favorite caf food?" is paying off.

"Yeah, but then maybe instead of taking the person's pic, we take a pic of their memory instead. So then in the end we'll have all these shots of Spalding icons, and maybe make it into some sort of collage?"

I nod. "We could get it printed on poster paper and make a massive mural for the gym wall," I say, nodding. "It's a great idea. We should make sure that people know their memory can be of anything while they were here at Spalding. Like Pete's Pizza, the car wash on DeMoines, which is always totally staffed by Spalding students every summer . . ."

I stop at the water fountain in the atrium to get a sip of water. Ben leans casually against the wall, one foot up. I stand up and tilt my head back, looking up to the bright afternoon sun that's coming in through the glass ceiling above us.

"Hold this a second," I say, pointing at the button for the fountain. Ben depresses the button, and I bend down so I'm eye level with the fountain, pulling my camera to my face.

I adjust the shutter speed to 1/125 and a narrow aperture to ensure the water droplets are in focus and then set my ISO to 100 to capture all the detail. I fire off a few shots, then check the viewfinder. Close, but not quite. I fine-tune the exposure and squat even lower, then try a few more times. "Got it."

"Let's see."

I show Ben the reflection of light on the stream of water, set against the stainless-steel backsplash.

"Not bad." He grins.

I roll my eyes at him. "I gotta go."

"So I'll tell Principal F our idea?"

"Wait. We should talk to the rest of photo club, see what they think . . ."

"Gemma's the only other one working on this with us."

"True, but . . ."

"She's totally going to be on board with this. I'll text her. Let's just pitch it to Forsythe and then we can get started."

"It's just . . ." I can feel myself blushing.

"What?"

"Listen." I look around to make sure no one's listening. "I don't want Dylan getting the wrong idea about us. I want it to be very clear that this is an assignment we *have* to do, because Principal F asked photo club to contribute. *Not* because you and I want to work together."

Ben looks momentarily stunned, then recovers. "Listen, I get it. You have a boyfriend. You chose him over me, like, months ago. There's nothing between us. I'm void of feelings when it comes to you. You're kind of just like this androgynous thing. Like a parakeet. But one of the smart ones, that can do tricks and talk and stuff. So don't stress."

Now I feel sort of silly.

"Do you want me to call Dylan and tell him there's nothing to worry about?"

"No, definitely *don't* do that. I'll tell him," I say, already dreading the conversation. But I'm relieved to hear Ben say it: there is nothing between us. I'm a parakeet.

"I look forward to our strictly Photo Club Business interactions," Ben says, seriously, sticking out his hand. I smile, shaking his hand.

"Don't smile!" he says as I pull open the door to the photocopy room. "Someone might actually think you're having fun with me."

CHAPTER 5

"Buckle up, we've got a long ride ahead of us," Dylan says when he picks me up shortly after 8 on Friday night. He's wearing a driving cap, which he moves out of the way to kiss me when I get in the car.

"We do?" I close the door of Dylan's Dadmobile and feel a flutter of excitement.

"Radio Flyers—the band that opened for Cherry Blasters?—are playing tonight at Roxy's. I can get us in and introduce you to the band."

"Oh," I say, trying to hide my disappointment. Dace and I had spent hours trying to figure out what Dylan's surprise would be. A hotel room for our first time? Dinner at a fancy restaurant? Tickets to some photography or art exhibit I don't know about? Worst-case scenario I guessed he would take me to the new Channing Tatum movie—the one he keeps making fun of me for wanting to see.

"I should probably check with my mom," I say, trying to keep my voice light as I text Mom. One of our first dates was a concert, so I don't know why I'm not excited to see a band tonight, except that it's a band Dylan spent two weeks with, and it feels like I'm tagging along to this other life he had, or something. A second later, Mom texts back, telling me to have fun. I'm surprised she's OK with the long-distance night out. I wonder if it's because I've been cold with her, and she's trying to get back on my good side.

Dylan's chattering about the Radio Flyers, filling me in on some development with all his band friends since he's been back, and the next thing I know he's repeating my name.

"Sorry. Zoned out for a sec," I say.

"So anyway, I was saying . . ." I know he's trying to make me feel connected to the band, to his new friends, but the more he goes on about them, the more disconnected I feel.

"You OK?" he says, and I nod.

"I'm sure the band will be great. I just . . . haven't heard them before, you know, so it's hard for me to be as excited to see them play. But I'm sure they'll be great." My face hurts from forcing a smile.

"Oh, I'll put them on right now," he says, grabbing his phone from the console between our seats. A second later, jangly guitars fill the air.

"They're awesome, right? You'll love the guys." He merges onto the freeway. "Actually, I should've told you what we were doing. Dace would've loved it too. She could've come along."

"Dace is at ski club." The clock on the dashboard glows green. Right about now they're skiing under the lights, weaving in and out of glistening trees. Or hot-chocolate-breaking inside the chalet by a fire. He doesn't say anything. "I wanted to join too, but you know, Fridays are supposed to be our night. When we do something we both want to do," I add.

Dylan glances over at me. "Was that a dig?"

"No," I lie.

"If you want to join ski club, join ski club."

I want him to add, "But I'd miss you." Or "We can find another night to have date night." Something that indicates he still wants one night to be our night. But he doesn't. Neither of us says anything for a while. He's tapping on his steering wheel to the beat of the song as though nothing's wrong, and I try to shake off my bad mood. How was he supposed to know I didn't want to go see the Radio Flyers? And it's just one Friday. One Friday in a lifetime of Friday night dates. And Dylan and I are together—and we always have fun, no matter what we're doing. I just need to stop overthinking it. Dylan cranks the radio, catches my eye and sticks out his tongue at me and I laugh. I lean back in my seat as he roars down the freeway.

● ● ●

It's a little after 9 when we get to Roxy's, but the bar is already packed. Everyone at Spalding talks about Roxy's, but almost no one has actually gotten in, since the bouncers are renowned for being total hard-asses about fake ID. But Dylan's on the guest list and one of the Radio Flyers guys is standing at the door talking to the bouncer when we get to the door, and he looks at us, nods, and like that, we're in. Dylan shakes hands with the Radio Flyers guy, says something to me that I can't hear over the noise and then grabs my hand and pulls me through the throngs of people, as though he knows exactly where he's going. I bite my lip and stare intently at everyone's shoes.

"DM! DM! DM!"

This gaggle of girls is suddenly standing beside us, though one stands out—she's got jet-black hair, big bangs, bright red full lips, the kind that hold lipstick perfectly—and she practically leaps into Dylan's arms, hugging him tight, and I'm left there, staring, mouth agape.

When they break apart, Dylan looks from the girl, to me, and then slings his arm around me, which makes me feel *slightly* better about the love-in that just happened before my eyes. Then the girl backs up, if only slightly, to resume her spot with her three friends.

"Muse, this is Pippa." He squeezes my shoulder.

"Hey," Muse says, tilting her head, broadly grinning and throwing her hand out to me.

Muse? Her name is Muse? I try to remind myself it's just a name and doesn't mean she's as fascinating as her name sounds. But she *looks* fascinating. She's got a tattoo that runs the length of the inside of her arm from her wrist to her elbow. It says something—in swirly font—but I can't read what.

"It's great to meet you," she says to me. "I've

heard *so* much. You're even prettier in person," she says. I don't know where to start. She's heard so much about me? When? Where? I've heard nothing about her. Why is she being so *nice*? Why do I want to hate her?

"And it's soooo good to see you," Muse says, smiling at Dylan. Her eyes are the kind that sparkle. The kind you can't take your own eyes off. "Texting just isn't the same."

I look from her to Dylan, who looks . . . oblivious. He's been texting with Muse? Dylan just nods, as I try to figure out who this girl is.

"We'll grab drinks," Dylan says. "Want something?"

"Oh, no thanks, we've got a pitcher over there," she says, pointing to the table behind her, where her three friends have disappeared to. "But come over, we'll grab you seats."

"Cool." He turns and I follow him to the bar, even though 98% of me wants to just walk right back out the door of the club.

"What do you want?" He asks.

"Just a Coke," I say, and he orders one and himself a club soda.

"How do you know her?" I ask after he hands me the glass and clinks his with mine. He takes a sip of his drink.

"Muse? She was on the tour."

"She was? Like every show?" This might've been useful information. But what was he supposed to tell me, that he was hanging out with this gorgeous girl for two weeks? I can see why it didn't come up.

Dylan takes another sip of his drink and looks

around, bobbing his head to the music playing over the PA. He turns to me and says something I can't hear and points to the table where Muse is, and I follow him. He downs the rest of his soda as he walks ahead of me and puts his cup down on a table as we pass. Muse eyes Dylan and jumps up as we approach. She leans close, saying something to him, her cheek pressed to his cheek. I'm behind him, so I can't see his reaction to whatever she's saying. She sits back down, pulling a chair closer to her, for him. But he grabs another chair for me, and puts the two empty ones together, and then we sit and he leans over to tell me the band should be on any minute, and I nod, then focus on the straw in my drink.

If only I had my camera here. Seeing the night through the lens, focusing on everything from behind my camera, giving me something else to do so I'm not just stuck in this awkwardness.

"Want a beer?" one of Muse's friends offers. I shake my head, but Dylan nods and takes the plastic cup.

"You're drinking?" Dylan never used to drink, because of the cancer and the treatments. And even though he's cancer-free now, he didn't tell me he was drinking.

"Not a big deal, OK?" he says, not looking at me. "I know you can't drive us home—I'm just having one."

"Does Muse know about the cancer?" I blurt out as the band comes onstage.

Dylan gives me an annoyed look. Brow furrowed, almost as though he's willing me to shut up without saying anything. "No. Nobody does." He takes a sip of his beer and looks back at the Radio Flyers as they kick into their first song.

I follow Dylan's gaze, toward the stage, but I'm distracted by Muse, who's jumped up and is dancing, shaking her hips in her black jeans, shimmying in her boots, throwing her hands in the air. When the song ends she whistles and then sits down, breathless. But when the next song starts, she's up again and so are her friends, and Dylan's pulling me to my feet. The song is catchy, but it's my first time hearing it, and they know all the words. I couldn't feel more out of place. I keep hoping each song is their last, but it never is, for more than an hour and a half, until finally, *finally* they call it quits.

I can't get out of there quick enough, but Dylan wants to say hi to the band, so it's another agonizing half hour until we're on the road. And the ride home—just the two of us—isn't any better. Dylan hits Radio Flyers on his iPod, and the now-familiar tracks make me replay the evening.

"When Mike K stood on his drum kit with the cast on his leg? Who does that?" he says, in that way when you admire someone who's clearly nuts.

"I guess that's how he got the broken leg?" I say.

"Yeah, two shows in." Dylan laughs. "That guy's so insane."

I don't laugh with him. "So you hung out with Muse the whole time you were away?"

"Yeah," he says, not adding any sort of amendment like, *But hey! She's gay!* Or *But don't worry, she's got a boyfriend!* Or even, *Yeah, there was absolutely no one else to hang out with, and I talked about you the whole time.* He merges onto the I-90 and the rest of the drive home he sings along with the Flyers and rehashes the night some more.

"Hey, so are you nervous about tomorrow?" I interrupt.

He glances over at me and I feel like a buzzkill, but also like I need to talk about something real—and other than the Radio Flyers. He shrugs, then turns his attention back to the road. "Nah. It's just a routine MRI. I have to get them every three months for two years or something."

He pulls off the highway and the playlist ends, and we revert to our mildly awkward mutual silent treatment. Eventually he pulls onto my street and into my driveway and turns off the car. Then he leans over and looks at me and I feel like I have his full attention for the first time all night. "Come here." He unbuckles my seatbelt and I twist in my seat toward him. He puts one hand on my knee and the other on the back of my neck and the warmth from his hands sends sparks throughout my body. And then his lips are on mine, and I'm closing my eyes and forgetting about the whole not-so-wonderful night. His breath is a mix of beer and minty gum and I stop thinking. I love kissing him.

"Philadelphia Greene," he says, when we finally pull apart, my curfew alarm dinging on my phone.

"What?" Our eyes meet.

"You are something else."

My stomach flip-flops. "I'll see you in the morning." He kisses me once more, and I don't want to get out of the car but I slide out and into the cold. I hurry up the steps and inside, locking the door behind me.

CHAPTER 6

Dylan parks in the visitor lot, and we make our way up the concrete stairs to the front door of St. Christopher's early Saturday morning. These steps hold mixed feelings—that panic attack the first time I returned to the hospital after Dad's death, but also, the first time Dylan and I met. Or re-met, since he'd graduated.

"Wait a sec," I say as Dylan's about to walk through the sliding doors. He turns. I race back down the stairs and then turn and crouch so that the railing along the left side of the stairs is at eye level, a leading line from the bottom left corner of the frame up to Dylan at the top.

"I better not be in these," he calls, amused.

I pull off a few more shots and then race back up the stairs. "It's for the alumni-dance mural thing I told you about. Favorite memories of Spalding."

"What, and I'm yours?" He grins.

"Obviously." The volunteer placement I had dreaded turned out to be the best thing that ever happened to me. I still have the other half of my hours to complete before graduation, but those hours start up again next fall, somewhere else. Though I can't imagine anywhere else comparing to my time at St. Christopher's, especially in the romance department.

The sliding doors open and the warmth envelops us, sucking us into the bright atrium, where it could be summer.

"Dylan," the receptionist says, and Dylan smiles. "And Pippa. We miss you around here. Especially when you were sneaking around to find Dylan."

I blush.

It's kind of cute how everyone knows we're together now, and we walk down the hall. We're just getting to the elevator when Luis Juarez, who graduated from Spalding last year, comes around the corner.

"Dylan! Where you been hiding?"

Dylan slaps his good hand—the other one is peeking out of a cast—but avoids his question. "You know Pippa?"

Luis gives a friendly smile. "I remember you." I nod.

"What happened?" Dylan asks. Luis holds the casted arm up.

"Snowmobile fail. Luckily it was my left so I should still be able to man the camera and even the boom pretty easily. We're shooting this mockumentary . . ." Luis, like the majority of last year's graduates who opted for the local community college, is taking the radio and television arts program. It's always the most popular. "So what are you guys doing here?"

"Pippa had to pick up something for school—for her volunteer placement," Dylan blurts out before I can say anything.

"Cool. Well, four hours in here is long enough for me. This place is depressing." He cocks his head. "Hey, my parents are out of town next weekend. So, party, obviously. See you there?"

"Yeah, maybe," Dylan says, noncommittally.

"Oh, too good for Spalding now, huh?" Luis teases, then salutes with his casted arm and walks past us, toward the main entrance.

I nudge Dylan. "Way to rope me into your lie," I say as we wait for the elevator.

Dylan has this thing about people knowing he got sick. Except for with me, his friend Callie and his parents and doctors, he fibs all the time to cover for it. Although, it's not like he was exactly on the up and up with me either when we first starting hanging out here at the hospital.

The elevator's empty and we get on. His expression is unreadable, and I know he's more nervous about this test than he's willing to admit. The doors open and Dylan is out into the hall. He picks up his pace and I have to practically jog to keep up with him.

My gut feels like it's full of rocks.

I grab Dylan's hand and squeeze it. We turn down a hall and then down another, lots of people saying hi to Dylan and him responding with a fake smile, until we end up in the waiting room for the MRI.

I don't recognize the woman at the desk—she must have started after my placement ended, and she doesn't know Dylan either. He gives his name and hospital card, and she types something into the computer and hands the card back and tells him that it'll just be a moment. We move over to sit in one of the black chairs that line the walls of the waiting room.

Dylan pulls out his phone.

"Hey, don't you find it kind of exhausting to keep up the lies?" I say quietly. "Why not let it go after these results?"

"I just don't want the world to know about it," he whispers hoarsely.

"But there's not even really anything to know. You don't have cancer anymore. You beat it. It's awesome. You should be happy that people know. It's inspiring."

"Yeah, real accomplishment. Take a bunch of drugs and lie on the couch for weeks. Listen, I don't want to talk about it, OK?"

He refocuses on his phone, and I peek over his shoulder at his screen.

"You have 2,916 Instagram followers? I didn't even know you Instagrammed." I say incredulously.

He shrugs. "I took this pic backstage one night with the Blasters, and now, like, all their followers are following me."

"Huh." I open the Instagram app and search for him by name. DylMc—*DylMc?*—has a lot of photos. And a certain *MuseMusicLove* has liked a lot of them. I keep scrolling. Actually, Muse has liked every single one of his photos. Even ones—a pic of his toes?—that are really not worth liking. His phone dings and he laughs, types something, then puts his phone in his pocket and looks at me, catching me watching him.

"What?"

"Nothing," I say. But of course I want to know if it's Muse he's texting.

"OK."

I know it's not the time—he's about to have a "Has my cancer returned?" test—but I want to push it, tell him that no, I'm not OK, I think Muse is into him, and I need reassurance that nothing is going on between them, especially since I'm the one who's sitting here with him at the hospital. He grabs a magazine off the table—*Popular Mechanics*, which, what are *popular* mechanics? And more importantly, when did Dylan become interested in them?—and so I grab the only other magazine on the table, which is the *American Journal of Proctology*. If I'd known Dylan was going to basically ignore me, I would've brought a book to read. I'm only halfway through *The Scarlet Letter*, which we're supposed to be finished reading by Monday. Anything would be much better than reading about butt issues.

"Dylan McCutter?" A woman in a white lab coat over a purple sweater dress is standing in the hallway between the intake desk and the room where the MRI happens.

Dylan stands up. "Back soon."

I'm about to say "Good luck" but that seems inappropriate, so at the last second I jump up and kiss him on the lips, which sort of ends up half on his bottom lip and half on his chin. And then I sit right back down and Dylan heads toward the MRI technician, who smiles kindly and then leads him down the hall.

The hospital received a large donation last year and now the MRI room is like something out of *Star Trek*. The room doesn't have a door—just a massive wall you go around and then behind, which supposedly is a psychological trick. Like if you went into a room with doors, it would be like going to the other side, the *cancer* side, or something. On the wall, there's this huge light-up sign that says *In Use* in red letters. I watch as Dylan disappears behind the wall.

"The waiting's the worst," a voice says. An old man sits down beside me. He's holding a Bible. I nod, suddenly feeling the weight of what's happening. Dylan won't have the results today—the scan begins a morbid chain letter: the technician sends the scan to a specialist, who reads it, who then sends it to Dylan's doctor, who then calls Dylan in to let him know the results.

"Your brother?" the man asks.

"Boyfriend," I say.

"So young to have a boyfriend," he says, almost wistfully.

"I'm 16."

"I was 17 when I met my Margaret. We'll be married 70 years next month. We've been through it all, but love is blind, right?" He nods. "So's Margaret, now. Both eyes and still has to get treatment to make sure it doesn't spread even further. I read the Bible. Mostly to pass the time, and because I can still see. Have you read it?" he asks, as though he's holding up the latest bestseller everyone's talking about.

I shake my head. "I'm not . . . really religious. We don't go to church. Except for weddings and funerals, I guess."

"Me either, but this—it's a pretty good story. Told four ways. It's a little like reading a court transcript for a very juicy trial. There's murder and adultery. I'm quite into it." He pats the cover. "I'm hoping her treatments are done before I finish, and I never find out how it all ends." He winks at me.

The In Use sign clicks off; Dylan will be out any minute. I stand to get a drink of water, and when I come back Dylan emerges. He grins at me. "I feel a bit like a superhero when I'm in there. Like the Incredible Hulk getting radiated." He laughs. I figured he'd be thinking about cancer and death in that room, but he looks like a weight's been lifted.

"You ready?" Dylan grabs his coat and hat off the seat beside me. I say goodbye to the old man and follow Dylan through the double doors.

"What was the percentage of recurrence again?" I ask once we're out in the hallway, waiting for the elevator, even though I know the answer. The chance of his cancer coming back is low—4%. But I ask to remind him. To keep the mood light in case his superhero act isn't that solid. He rolls his eyes at me—he knows what I'm trying to do.

"Let's go get something to eat. I'm starving. Caf?"

"Seriously?" We haven't eaten in the caf since I was a candystriper and he was a patient. Back when I didn't know he was sick, when I thought he was on the nonexistent music team, and we would pick out the most awful-looking foods, just to prove something doesn't have to look good to taste good.

"Actually, that's probably a bad idea, right?" He grabs my hand and leads me down the hall, around a corner and straight for a set of doors that says *Open Only in Emergency. Alarm Will Sound.* He looks at me, grins and pushes open the door, then pulls me through as the siren blares. We race down the stairs, two at a time. He's whooping. I'm laughing and suddenly everything feels all right again.

CHAPTER 7

For seven years, Sleepover Saturdays have been Dace and my thing, but as I'm lying on my bed on Saturday afternoon, post-hospital escape, wasting time online when I should be editing my photos for photo club, Dace texts to cancel. She thinks she has the flu. Actually, what she texts is this:

Dace: 99% sure I have flu. Or Lyme disease. Possible spider bite on arm.

Me: Lyme disease caused by ticks not spiders.

Dace: Maybe spider flu then?

Me: U sure it's not bird flu?

Dace: OMG is that a thing?

Me: No. Well yes. But no way u have it.

Dace: What if I got it in biology?

Me: Weren't u dissecting worm?

Dace: What if bird touched worm & I touched
worm & now have rare disease? Will I be
better by tomorrow?

She has a go-see tomorrow for the Nordstrom
website. Catalog work isn't what she wants to do,
but since her agent used to book her for car shows
in Cheektowaga, this is a lot better.

I tell her to eat a lot of Arrowroots and that I
love her. She tells me if she dies I can have her bras.
Then I call Dylan to see if he wants to do something.
After going to the Orange Turtle, this diner we kind
of made our place over the holidays, he dropped
me off at home, saying he had to help his dad chop
firewood. I figure he should be done by now. He
answers his phone on the second ring.

"I'm going to the Radio Flyers' second show,
remember? Aren't you sleeping at Dace's?"

I flop on my bed and tell him Dace is sick and
wait for him to say he doesn't need to see the band
he saw for two weeks straight and then again last
night and would rather see me, but he doesn't. I try
not to be disappointed that he is sticking to his plan.
Of course, I made it clear to Dylan that Sleepover
Saturdays were a tradition and I didn't want to
become one of those girls who forgets all about her

best girlfriends the second she gets a boyfriend. So I can't exactly expect him to drop his plans just because my plans changed.

Then, almost as though he can hear my thoughts, he says, "Do you want to come?" But I don't. Last night was fine, except for the entire four hours where I felt totally inferior to Muse and paranoid that there was something going on between them. So a repeat performance? No thanks.

"Is Muse going to be there?" I ask, regretting it the second the question leaves my lips. I sound unmistakably jealous.

"Yeah, probably," he says. "She goes to all the shows. You know she's Patrick's girlfriend, right?"

Silence. "What?"

"Patrick, the bassist."

It's like the sky has opened up and there's rainbows and butterflies *everywhere*.

"Oh! Great!" I can't control my enthusiasm.

"I told you that."

He *did?*

And then it all clicks together—how he told me he was hanging out with some of the girlfriends of the bands. He never said their names, though. And I figured they were all about their semi-famous boyfriends and weren't thinking about Dylan in *that* way because even though I know he's a super-talented musician, to those girls I figured they just thought he was the dude in the merch booth.

"You're a freak," Dylan teases, and then tells me he'll call me tomorrow.

I'm making myself a Nutella sandwich when Mom's phone rings. She's upstairs, so I peek at it. My heart stops.

David Westerly.

The knife in my hand shakes and I put it down on the counter and then wipe my hands on my jeans just as the phone stops ringing and it goes to voicemail.

One Missed Call.

A moment later the phone dings, and the voicemail icon pops up. I pick up her phone, my hands quivering.

Why is David calling Mom? Is this a random one-off or are they talking now? "Was that my phone?" Mom calls down the stairs. A creak escapes my lips when I open my mouth. I clear my throat, wondering what to say. My heart's pounding. But then I march up the stairs. She's in her room, sorting through her closet.

I toss her phone on the bed.

"It was David Westerly. You're talking to David Westerly?" I practically spit out the words.

She turns, holding a dark purple sweater. She glances at the phone and then back to me. "Why are you using that tone?"

"So yes?"

She sighs. "Yes."

"Were you going to tell me?"

"It wasn't a secret," she says slowly. "You and I

haven't exactly been chatty lately. And he's been friends with your father for years."

"Mom, you can stop the charade now. He's my *birth father*, and you pretended you never liked him. You didn't talk to him for my *entire life* and now you are? Or have you been talking to him all these years and I just didn't know?"

"No, of course not. David was your father's friend. We made the decision that that would be the relationship to uphold. Pippa, after what he did, I didn't want anything to do with him."

"So why now?"

"He called after your father died, and every once in a while he calls to check on me. While you were in New York, he let me know how you were doing a few times."

"If you wanted to know how I was doing you could've just asked me."

"Sweetie, why are you so upset? I haven't told him that you know he's your father."

"He's *not* my father. I don't *want* David in my life. I don't *need* David in my life. And as far as I can tell, you've been doing fine without him all this time. I don't get why you need to talk to him now." Only, as soon as I say it, it dawns on me. This isn't even about me. What if this is about her? What if now that Dad is gone, she's thinking, What if? What if she wants to sub in David for Dad?

She sits down on the bed and pats a spot on the floral comforter beside her but I shake my head. It's not the only thing shaking.

"Have you given any more thought to telling

him?" she asks. "I think he has a right not to be the only one left in the dark."

I shake my head. "I can't believe you're still going on about this. I knew I never should've told you."

She looks like I've slapped her. "You wouldn't have kept that from me."

"You kept it from me." I cross my arms over my chest, then mumble, "I wish I had."

She stands. "Pippa, you don't mean that." Her voice is annoyingly calm, but she looks like she might cry, and it makes me crazy—I'm the one who gets to be upset here.

I throw my hands up. "Are you kidding? Of course I do. If I'd never told you, we wouldn't be having this conversation. We could just go on like we were."

"Pretending."

"Exactly. Pretending like you did for 16 years." Our eyes lock. "Lying to me."

"I—we—did it to protect you. And to protect your relationship with your father."

"You *lied* to me." I move toward the door and grip the round handle. "David doesn't care if I know he's my father. He doesn't want to be my father. Also he's a total womanizing man-whore. I can't believe you ever fell for him."

"Pippa, stop it. You know he said—"

"I don't want to know what he said."

"You have a choice: either you can tell him or I—"

"That's not a choice, it's an ultimatum." I storm out of her room, slamming the door behind me.

Worst Saturday night ever.

CHAPTER 8

Later in the week, Principal Forsythe announces to the school that because the alumni events fall on the same weekend as Valentine's Day, there'll be only one dance—for everybody. Most people think it's a terrible idea—old people like my mom at the same dance as us?—but it means that Dylan will be at the dance. Our first school dance together as BF-GF. The other part of his announcement: alumni bands are invited to play a three-song set onstage in the gym.

"I think there are limited spots, so you should sign RFBR up soon," I tell Dylan, referring to his old band Rules for Breaking the Rules. We're sitting on the basement couch watching TV after school. Mom is upstairs in the kitchen. We've barely said two words to each other all week.

Dylan shakes his head. "Yeah, maybe."

I once read if you say "Yes" but you shake your

head no, subconsciously you're saying no. It's as though you can lie, but your body language tells the truth.

He flicks the remote.

"Maybe?" I press.

"Those guys don't want to play some dumb high school dance."

"It's not a high school dance, it's an alumni reunion. They're saying everyone who ever went to Spalding will be coming back for it. It's a big deal."

"You know what's a big deal?" He grins at me. "My parents are away this weekend . . ."

"They are?"

"Yes. They leave Saturday morning." He puts a hand on my knee and raises his eyebrows. I glance toward the stairs, then shimmy a little closer to him.

"So . . . ?" I whisper in his ear.

"So." He runs his hand up my leg, then turns his face toward me and our lips meet. Tingles run up my leg and I feel warm all over. His kisses get me right in the stomach. Eventually we break apart. "Hmm, what were we watching?" he asks, nodding at the TV. A car commercial is playing.

"No clue."

"Ha. Want something to drink?"

"Sure, water."

As soon as he's out of the room, I grab my phone and text Dace.

Me: Dylan's parents=away this wknd.

Dace: FAREWELL VIRGINIA TOUR!

Dace is obsessed with calling my virginity "Virginia."

Me: Can I get free pass on Sleepover Saturday this wk?

I feel guilty as I wait for her response.

Dace: OK. But aren't we doing Luis's party?

I'd actually forgotten all about the party. Then it hits me why Dace has remembered—and why she wants to go.

Me: Ohhhh . . . how did I not see this one coming?

Dace: Yeah yeah, so obvs.

Dace has this rule about dating guys: they must be older than her and not go to our school. Which means Luis is a perfect fit.

Dylan comes back down the stairs with two glasses of water and a bag of chips in his mouth. "Your mom knows the way to a boyfriend's heart," he says when he's dropped the chips in my lap.

I take a sip of water and put the glass on the coffee table. "Luis Juarez's party is Saturday. Dace wants to go, and if I'm going to bail on Sleepover Saturday, I should go too. But we could go for a bit, right? It'll be fun to go to a party together."

"Fun?" He raises his eyebrows and opens the bag

of salt 'n' vinegar chips. He pops a couple of chips in his mouth as his phone dings. He grabs it, laughs and texts something back. When he looks up, his eyes meet mine.

"Sorry." He puts his phone—face down—on the table.

I raise my eyebrows. "What's so funny?"

"There was this super fan at a show, and Muse and I keep saying this thing he said. It's not even funny—it's dumb."

It may be dumb, it may not be funny, but it feels important. He has inside jokes with her. My face falls and I bite my lip.

"Hey, remember when you used to text *me*?" I try to keep my tone light, but I can't keep out the edge.

"My love for you runs deeper than a meaningless text. And besides, you were just texting Dace."

Ugh, boyfriends. Texting your best friend and texting some hot girl (even if she has a BF) are not the same thing. Dylan pulls me close and then tilts my face toward his and kisses me, square on the lips. And even though I close my eyes, all I can picture is Dylan smiling at his phone. The way I always thought he smiled when he got a text from me. Does he smile that same way when anyone texts? Do his eyes dance that way for everyone? Or is there something about Muse?

Dylan must sense me stiffening up because he pulls away and looks at me.

"Sorry," I say, but I'm not sorry, not really.

"What's up with you? You're not being your normal lovable self."

"Nothing." I sigh. "I guess I'm just grumpy." I lower my voice. "Maybe it's Mom stuff."

"Why? She seems fine," he says. As though giving him chips makes everything in my life right again? I want him to put his arms around me and tell me he'll squeeze the bad mood out of me, but instead, he says, "Wanna call it a night?"

"Sure," I say, when what I want to say is "No, don't go."

He kisses me on the top of the head. "Let's talk about it tomorrow or something, when your Mom's not at the top of the stairs. Love you, Pip."

"Love you too," I say, feeling dejected. I sit on the couch until I hear the front door close, and then I go upstairs.

"Dylan left early," Mom calls from the kitchen.

"Mm-hmm," I say from the hallway, my hand on the banister.

"Everything OK?"

I can see Mom standing at the mixer. We used to always bake together after school, back when Dad was still alive and Mom was home all the time. It felt so easy to talk about what was bugging me. I want to ask her what she's baking, if I can help. But I can't bring myself to. It feels like giving in.

"I'm going to edit," I say, heading up the stairs. I slump on my bed and stare at the ceiling.

I'm still so angry with her. It sucks, because through everything—Ben stealing my photos, my panic attacks, Dad dying, Dad being sick, having Reggie Stevenson dump me, failing my swimming lesson, peeing my pants in the second grade Christmas concert—Mom has been there. On my side. Always the one I turned to. And now, it feels like there's this awful divide between us. It feels like if I lean on her at all, I'm giving in on the David thing. Just because someone is technically your biological father doesn't make him your dad. I turn on my side to look at my custom wallpaper, focusing in on a pic of my dad and me when I was a baby. What if I give in and she takes that as my blessing?

I get up and go to my desk, flip open my laptop and open Photoshop. After going through all my possible options for this week's photo club and narrowing the group down to a select few, I grab my phone to text Dylan.

Me: Sorry about tonight.

I pause, waiting to see if he's going to respond. When he doesn't, I decide to give myself an at-home spa treatment as a distraction—a reason to ignore my phone for 20 minutes. I turn on the old baseboard heater in the bathroom, which makes the small room toasty in minutes, and run the water in the tub. I slather my face with a mud mask and my hair with a double dose of conditioner and then soak until my toes are raisin-like. After quenching my skin in vanilla body butter, I rewrap myself in my towel to go into the hall. The glow of Mom's bedside light peeks out from under her door, but I go back to my room, put on my favorite pajamas and crawl into bed.

My phone dings.

Ben: You awake?

Me: Yeah.

Ben: Check out Spalding Facebook page. I posted asking alumni for fave memories and there's got to be at least 100 already.

Me: Wow, great idea.

Ben: Yeah, occasionally I get a good one. Hey also! Check out the moon. It's a supermoon.

The blinds are covering my window, and I pull them aside. The moon looks like someone put a sepia effect on it.

Me: It's hard to text back wonderment.

Ben: Incredible isn't it? It's called perigee-syzygy.

Me: How do u know that?

Ben: Magic of Wikipedia. Anyway, g'nite.

Me: Night.

I grab my camera from my desk, then fiddle with the aperture. I set my camera on the windowsill so it's steady. Crouching down, I look through the viewfinder at the moon, then aim and start snapping photos. It's hard to get the shot right, especially since I still can't help but listen for my phone to ding, wondering when Dylan will text back, and my heart's only half in it.

CHAPTER 9

"Whose house is the party at again?" Mom asks as I come down the stairs. She's stretched out on the couch doing a crossword puzzle. I tell her. "OK. And you're sleeping at Dace's?"

I could say yes and she'd never know any different. But instead, I open up a big can of boyfriend worms.

"Dylan's parents are away, actually. We're gonna go to the party together, then he wants me to sleep over."

She puts the crossword down on the coffee table and swings her legs around so she's sitting up. She studies me.

"So I'll probably do that." My heart's pounding as I grab my coat out of the front hall closet. After pulling it on, I sit down on the bottom step of the stairs to put my boots on, which drives my mom crazy because it gets muck on the carpet. But she doesn't say anything about it this time.

She comes over, is about to say something, stops, then exhales loudly. "I'm glad you told me the truth."

I bite my lip and nod. "Yeah. Well."

She sits beside me on the bottom stair. My shoulders feel weighed down by my coat.

"I knew we'd talk about this at some point. I just didn't . . ." She trails off. "Are you sure you're ready?"

I nod. "I'm ready, and I'm *ready*," I say, standing and grabbing my hat, scarf and mitts out of my bag and pulling them on. She knows I've been on the pill for more than a year now because it helps with my cramps and acne, but we've also talked about how the pill is not enough and condoms are the only way to protect against diseases. She usually makes some sort of corny joke that mildly mortifies me, but she doesn't joke now.

Mom puts her hands on her knees. "Sex can be a lot of pressure. In any relationship."

I nod.

"Just . . . don't feel like you can't change your mind, even if you set out thinking tonight's the night, that you have to go through with it. You can always change your mind. There'll be other nights."

"I should go."

"I love you."

"I'll text you when I get back to Dylan's." I stand and sling my bag over my shoulder.

She stands too and follows me to the door. I pull it open, then turn to her. Despite everything, I feel like I can't continue to walk out the door without telling Mom I love her. Not with Dad gone. Not that Mom's even going anywhere, but . . . you just never know. "I love you too, Mom."

I walk down the snowy driveway, staring up at the starry sky. It's one of those calm winter nights. It's not that cold, there's no wind, and I've got time, so I walk slowly, taking the ravine route. The path is just lightly dusted with snow, like icing sugar on a chocolate cake. I pull my camera out of my bag, to capture this night on film and calm my nerves at the same time. The path winds, leading me into the scene through the lens, and then, every so often, the path forks, creating a V, one route heading back to an easement between the houses and then out to the street. I pause at the fifth fork and crouch down, then pull my camera up to my face, focusing on the lines of the path, leading from the bottom of the photo up to the two top corners of the viewfinder. Then I head out the easement onto Dylan's street.

Dylan's house is dark when I get there, and when he opens the door I can just see a flicker of light coming from the living room behind him. My toes tingle; he's probably made the space super romantic, with candles.

"Hey," he says, opening the door wider. He's wearing a plaid button-down and jeans, and just looking at him makes me nervous, like it's our first date or something, and I wonder if he feels the same way. The sound of cheers escapes the living room and I realize there's no dreamy candlelit scene happening, but the TV turned to a sports channel.

Still, when he leans in to kiss me, I feel like, *Yes,*

this is it. We are on track. He pulls away and grabs my hands in his. "Wanna go upstairs?"

Right down to business, I think. I kick off my boots, then follow him upstairs, my heart racing.

His room is dark, but everything's different from a few days ago when I was here. He's moved his bed over to underneath his window, and all his basket-ball and baseball trophies that were on his shelves are gone. In fact, the shelves are gone too. Instead, that wall is filled with band posters and a signed Cherry Blasters T-shirt. Which he must've gotten on the road. I used to think of Cherry Blasters as our band, since it was our first concert together, but now, it sort of feels like his two-week tour with the band has trumped that; it's his thing now.

"You moved things around," I say, noticing his guitar in the corner, foot pedals lining one wall. It truly looks like a musician's room now. It's cool, for sure, but it feels like a bit less of the Dylan I knew, who once brought me into his room and showed me the space he'd had since he was seven. It was a glimpse into who he was and what made him who he is now. The guy not everyone else gets to see. But this, this feels like exactly the Dylan he's portraying out there in the world. There's no secret left for me.

"Yeah, just got rid of all that babyish stuff, you know."

Dylan fiddles with his laptop and music comes out through the speakers on his desk. And then he moves toward me and pulls me in, kissing me. He smells like soap, in the best possible way.

I put my hands on his hips and close my eyes,

trying to lose myself in the moment. His hands move to the bottom of my striped shirt, and he slips them under, lifting my shirt over my head. My shirt drops to the ground and he fiddles with my zipper. I push my jeans down around my ankles and sit on the bed to remove them, as he undoes his pants.

He doesn't say anything about my matching underwear, which feels a little discouraging. But who cares if my underwear match? Except that I spent a week's worth of Scoops wages I'd been saving from last summer for college on the black and coral set, which Dace helped me pick out over the holidays. In preparation.

Dylan pulls his shirt over his head and then sits down on the bed beside me and runs a hand over my leg, which sends chills up it. I put a hand on his leg too and then we're lying on the bed and we're kissing each other all over and he's running his hands over me, through my hair, down my arms, touching my breasts, skimming his hands lightly over my stomach, until he's touching the top of my underwear.

He kisses me harder and then pulls me on top of him, but I can feel he's not into it. I run my hands over his arms and try to kiss him more passionately, but the more I try to think about being the World's Sexiest Kisser to get him into it, the less into it I feel. And he's still not responding down there. Finally he pulls away and sits up.

"Don't be embarrassed," I say, putting my hand on his forearm, not knowing what else to say. But I'm embarrassed. This isn't supposed to happen, is it? Is it me? Or is it something else? What if the cancer's back and this is a side effect? "Did you get the results of your MRI?"

He stiffens. "Jesus, Pippa." He shakes his head like he's genuinely confused why I would bring up the Big C the middle of our Capital S sexy times. "The results were fine. I would've told you if they weren't." He pushes himself up and off the bed and goes into the bathroom. I sit there, in my bra and underwear on the bed, kind of cold, and kind of weirded out, and mad at myself for ruining the moment. I hear water running in the bathroom and I'm not sure what to do. Should I stand up? Should I get under the covers? Just keep lying here, half naked? I swing my legs over the end of the bed and grab his plaid button-down, slipping my arms through it and buttoning it up. This is cute. And I'm less freezing. He comes back in, and the long hair that usually sweeps across his face is wet, like he's splashed water on his face. He grabs his jeans off the floor and pulls them on, then looks at me. "Oh. I, uh, I was going to wear that shirt," he says.

I feel the heat rising up, out the neck of his shirt and I yank it off and hand it to him, mortified.

He pulls it on and begins buttoning it.

"We should get to the party, right?"

●　●　●

"So?" Dace practically jumps on me when we get to Luis's house. He lives in Spalding Heights, the posher side of Spalding, and only went to Spalding High because he used to live on the normal side of the city until his dad's sandwich chain became the hottest thing since sliced bread, which, incidentally they use to make their sandwiches. The house is sprawling and set back from the road, with gates that open to let you into the winding driveway, which was already packed with cars when Dylan and I pulled in. Inside, there's got to be at least a hundred people, maybe more. Within seconds though, Dace spots me, and Dylan gets cornered by some seniors who probably thought he was a big deal last year.

"Dylan, where the hell have you been, man?" someone yells from halfway up the circular staircase.

He shoots me a look that says, *This is why I didn't want to come.* As though I forced him. Technically, he's the one who put his pants on and ended the pre-party. I really don't get what the big deal is if people know that he had cancer, especially now that he doesn't. Sometimes it's too much pressure that I know and no one else does, except Dace of course, which is only more stress to make sure she doesn't blab to anyone.

"Someone's not in a very good mood," Dace says, cocking her head Dylan's way. She grabs my hand and drags me off to the kitchen.

When we get there, she hands me a red plastic cup and tells me to drink. I take a sip, make a face and then put the cup down.

"Tell me everything."

"It was, um, OK." I look around. Ben's in the corner, by a large aquarium, talking to Gemma. He catches my eye and raises his glass. I give a quick wave and turn back to Dace.

"OK? Are you kidding me? You had sex for the first time and it was OK?" She hisses. "Actually isn't that what people say? It's not that great? But still, I want *details*."

"Shhhhh!"

She shakes her head. "No one is paying any attention to us," but she pulls me out of the kitchen with its blaring music and through the dining room where a bunch of seniors are playing poker at the table, and then upstairs into one of—judging by the number of doors off the hallway—a dozen bedrooms. The first one is occupied and someone throws a shoe at Dace's head. She ducks, laughs and pulls me into the gleaming bathroom, closing the door behind us and locking it. "OK, deets."

I sit down on the marble floor, my back against the door. "Well. We didn't really do it."

There's silence. Dace perches on the edge of the Jacuzzi tub. "You didn't *really* do it? What does that even mean?"

"Fine, we didn't do it. It just didn't work . . . out." I inspect my coral nail polish, which matches my new underwear.

"*What* didn't work out? You're being incredibly cryptic. What are you talking about?"

"I don't know. It was super awkward and he wasn't *into* it—" I make a little fluttering hand gesture down there, and Dace's eyes widen. "And then I got all freaked out and then I asked him about his MRI results and he went into the bathroom and I wasn't sure what he was doing in there and then he came out and then we came to the party."

Dace is frozen. Then she blinks a bunch of times. "Holy rigatoni." She gets up and comes over to sit on the ground across from me and touches my arm gently. "OK." She pauses. "Definitely mortifying, but not insurmountable. It sounds like it was a whole bunch of factors. He was probably nervous, plus he knew you wanted to get to the party because you promised me, and then, OK, asking about the cancer thing was probably ill-timed. But maybe he was just thinking you'll do it after the party. When you're both loosened up a bit." She winks.

Someone bangs on the door.

"Hold your pants!" Dace calls then squeezes my shoulders. "You know what? The night's not over. It's only just beginning. We're gonna have some fun, we're gonna have a few drinks. We have to celebrate anyway—I got the Nordstrom job!"

"You did? That's great!" I say, feeling bad I didn't even ask her about it.

She waves a hand like it's nothing. "Things are going to work out. You're still sleeping at Dylan's tonight, right?"

I shrug. I don't even want to anymore.

"OK, let's go." She pops up and pulls me up, then produces a lipgloss from her back pocket and swipes it across my lips before I can protest. "There. A fresh stroke of lipgloss is like a reset. Now let's go have fun." She slides the tube in her back pocket and opens the door.

"Finally," some guy with a scruffy hipster beard says, exasperated. He pushes past us into the bathroom.

"We're playing Chug, Rush, Tell Your Crush," Gemma is announcing at the bottom of the stairs as we descend. She's holding two bottles of vodka like pompoms.

"We're in," Dace says, looking around.

Gemma heads toward the living room, telling everyone to follow her. She doesn't need to do much convincing. I pass Dylan, standing in the hall, his back against the wall and I stop and kiss him, then grab his hand. "Come on, this'll be fun." I'll tell Dylan he's my crush. It'll be cute and romantic. A moment.

"I'm gonna sit this one out," he says. "Or stand, actually." He pecks me on the cheek. He looks away.

"Why?"

He shrugs, and I can tell I've annoyed him, but I don't really know why.

"Hey, McCutter," some guy calls from the hallway, "we're watching the game in the basement. You in?"

"Yeah sure." He walks off and I turn and try not to be offended as I head into the living room and slide in between Dace and Emma, who are sitting cross-legged on the floor. Luis is cradling a stack of cups between his cast and chest and passing them out while Gemma explains the rules to everyone.

We go around a circle and when it's your turn you get a choice—chug from the bottle, do a rush dare (fraternity hazing style) or tell your secret crush that you're crushing on him or her.

"OK, me first!" Reggie Stevenson, the only other boyfriend I've ever had, says and Ben holds out the bottle to him.

"Chug, Rush, Tell Your Crush?"

"Chug, easiest." Reggie laughs and Ben pours the clear liquid into his cup. "Chug chug chug," someone chants and we all join in. Reggie throws back his Solo cup then slams it on the carpet, which is actually kind of ineffective since it's plastic. I can't believe I was ever into him. "OK, you're next," he says to Emma. "Chug, Rush, Tell Your Crush?"

"Rush." She has to have three pizzas delivered to her parents, cash on delivery.

We keep going around the circle. There are a bunch of other stupid rushes, including one where Alfred puts one of the tetra fish out of the aquarium in his mouth and then spits it back in the tank. "If Fishy Wishy dies I'm sending you the bill for the funeral," Luis's younger brother, Juan, jokes, and then it's Gemma's turn.

"Crush," she says, and Dace and I ooh, and then she pauses dramatically, takes a sip of whatever's in her cup and looks around the circle.

"Go on," someone teases.

"She's figuring out where he is," Dace defends Gemma. "Give her a second."

"I know where he is," she says, and then focuses in on someone across the circle. I follow her gaze.

"Ben." She cocks her head, holds up her cup and then takes another sip. I stare in shock. Dace nudges me, but I barely move. Ben lifts his cup in an across-the-circle cheers, then takes a sip.

Lisa, the editor of *Hall Pass*, who normally wouldn't even bother with one of these parties but started dating one of Luis's friends over the break, goes next. She chugs her Diet Coke and someone calls her on it, which I think is kind of a jerk thing to do, so I slap Dace on the knee and she knows instantly what I mean and we cheer for her, which I think makes her feel a bit better. And then it's my turn. I'm considering Chug because it's the safest, but you also get booed the most, but since everyone's gone easy on the girls who choose Rush, I go for it.

"Rush," I say.

"Kiss two guys in one night," Reggie says, raising his eyebrows.

"Um, I have a boyfriend, and he's here, so that would be weird," I say. Not to mention I don't want to kiss anyone else.

"How about a guy and a girl?" Dace says, leaning over and kissing me square on the lips. Reggie whoops. "I'm basically your forever boyfriend anyway," Dace says. Then she whispers in my ear. "Looks like someone's jealous." She raises her eyebrows and tilts her head and I look over at Ben. He's watching me, but he looks away, and then I look around the circle and notice Gemma's watching him.

Juan goes next, and asks Dace if she wants to go in the hot tub. Juan is a sophomore, and I don't know much about him, except that he's a cuter, more intense version of his brother, with dark smoldering eyes.

"Well, it's a Rush. I can't say no, right?" Dace says, and I'm surprised.

"Actually, it's a Crush," he says. Something happens between them, this instant, as Dace watches

Juan, like she's waiting for him to break the tension. He just looks at her, unwavering, and she swallows.

Instead of brushing him off, she flips her hair over her shoulder and tells him she'll go put on her bikini.

"Hot tub!" Reggie calls out and the game is unofficially over as everyone jumps up. I'm relieved.

"You can use my bedroom," Juan says to Dace. "Last door on the left."

"You'll come right?" she says to me and I nod, but I'm wide-eyed.

"What just happened over there?" I say. "That was intense."

"Which part?" she says, laughing as we head up the stairs.

The walls in Juan's room are navy, the carpet is too, and the furniture is all dark wood. There's a pile of clothes in the corner and a photo of some basketball player on his closet door. His desk has a bunch of textbooks piled high.

Someone knocks at the door, then opens it, and Dace holds her shirt over her naked chest.

"It's just me," Gemma says, poking her head around the door.

She looks at me, a bit like a frightened deer, and I roll my eyes. "Get in here."

She closes the door, and Dace resumes changing. "So um . . . about Ben," Gemma says. "I should've told you before. I just . . . well, I just couldn't really find the right time, and I didn't think anything would happen tonight or anything, but then . . . is this gonna be weird?" She sits on the edge of the bed. I search my bag for my bikini.

"No, it's fine, it's just . . . I didn't realize . . . I thought I was the only one who'd forgiven him for the whole iPod thievery thing."

"I know, right? But then you were talking about how he'd changed and it did seem like it, and we have English together and the alumni project and he's just so cute . . ." I pull my bikini bottoms on, then slip my top over my head and tie the strings.

"It's totally cool. Really. Awesome." I shove my clothes in my bag.

"Well," Dace says, clearing her throat loudly. "This has been sufficiently awkward. Are we ready?" Dace slings her towel over her blue and white striped bikini and I wrap mine around me, under my armpits, the way I do when I get out of the shower.

"Yes. Gemma, you coming too?" I ask.

"Sure, I'll just find my suit and change."

"OK, I'm just going to see if Dylan wants to come out," I say, heading down to the basement. "Meet you guys out back."

Dylan's sitting with a bunch of guys in the den. I hear enough to know he's talking about the Cherry Blasters tour. They're impressed, asking him question after question.

"Hey," I say, sidling up to him and kissing him on the cheek. "Wanna come in the hot tub?"

"Nah. Have fun."

I glance at the table, to the red cup that has just a bit of amber liquid left in it.

"Are you drinking?" I ask him.

"No."

I don't push him, but his breath smells like beer.

"You know, I actually think I'm gonna head pretty soon."

"Oh," I say, looking down at my towel. I hug it closer under my armpits. "I just put my bikini on."

He stands and slaps a few hands. "You want to stay?" he asks, as he heads up the stairs and I follow, securing the stupid towel that keeps loosening with each step.

The truth is, I do want to stay. But Dylan's parents are away. I should *want* to be with Dylan. This is our *chance*.

Dylan finds his coat from a ginormous pile of coats in the foyer. "Listen, I'm pretty tired," he says. "I'll probably just go to sleep."

"OK," I say. So does that mean I don't come over later? But I don't ask.

He kisses me on the nose. "Have fun," he says and then turns and he's out the door.

Out at the hot tub, Dace points to a spot beside her. I slide into the tub.

"Dylan just left."

"What the French fries is up with him?"

I bite my lip.

Two more girls get in the hot tub and I move closer to Dace and she shimmies closer to Juan, who puts his arm around her, and I don't want to bring Dace down with my Dylan drama when clearly *something is happening* with her and Juan.

Just then someone starts a snowball fight, and the party gets nuts. Everyone races out of the hot tub to join in, and within minutes, I'm laughing and screaming and freezing my feet off in the snow. And then we're piling back into the hot tub. Later we're huddled in our clothes around a fireplace in the den and drinking hot chocolate spiked with rum, and someone suggests strip poker but then a massive game of Twister happens before I lose anything other than my socks, and then we're watching retro videos and people start to either fall asleep or leave, so I stand at the door, gathering my stuff while Dace has a moment with Juan before Luis puts him in a head-lock and pulls him away. Dace sighs as we fall into step down the dark snowy street.

"Wait—was Juan the real reason you wanted to come to the party? Juan, not Luis?"

Dace sighs dramatically. "Yeah. Crazy, right? A year younger and he goes to our school. I'm breaking all my rules."

I laugh. "I think it's good to break your own rules once in a while."

"Want me to walk you to Dylan's?" Dace asks, but I realize it's the first time I've thought of Dylan since before the snowball fight. What does that mean?

I shake my head. "Can I sleep at your place?"

Dace hugs me. "Oh, honey bunches of oats," she says. "I thought you'd never ask."

CHAPTER 10

Mom's standing at the kitchen table folding the laundry I left in the dryer when I get home from Dace's. Dace was still snoring when I snuck out; even though it was barely 7, I couldn't sleep and was going crazy lying there. Dace and I made the mistake of scrolling through Instagram last night. Muse's latest post? A photo of a cookie smashed to bits with the caption: *My heart.* And now all I can do is let my imagination run rampant. Does Dylan have anything to do with why she's not with Patrick anymore?

I pour myself some orange juice and sit down at my usual seat.

"Well, how was the party?" Mom folds one of my sweaters and places it in the hamper.

"OK," I say, yawning.

"And Dylan's?"

I shrug. "I slept at Dace's."

She studies my face while I figure out how to play it. Then I notice something strange. "Are you wearing my jeans?"

There's my mom, in her mom hair, pulled back with a plastic headband, and a cable-knit sweater, neither of which manages to disguise her angular features and lithe figure, the look that got her in so many glossy magazine fashion spreads. And then, on the bottom, she's wearing my—yep, she's definitely wearing my dark wash Rock & Republic jeans. She's lost a lot of weight since Dad died. I hadn't noticed how much, until now.

"Oh," Mom says, looking down. "I just wanted to try them on, to see how these skinny jeans fit. Um, I thought, you know, maybe I'd buy myself a new pair of jeans. But jean shopping is just so daunting, and . . ."

The fact is she looks, like, hot. She's 40, but the jeans make her look like a cool 40. Definitely not the mom of a 16-year-old. And I can see that what my mom needs is for me to tell her she looks great, or she can borrow them, or that we should go shopping together, or something nice, but I can't bring myself to, not this morning. "I'm going to go garage saling," I say instead, downing the rest of my juice and getting up from the table.

"Oh," she says. "I was going to make waffles."

"Sorry Mom," I say, heading to the front door.

"I've got to work at noon," she calls after me. "Maybe we can watch a movie when I get home tonight?"

"Maybe," I say, checking my phone to see if

Dylan's texted back yet. I texted him before I went to sleep, just to say goodnight and that I was at Dace's. But my screen's blank.

I slip on my boots, my coat, a wool hat and fingerless gloves for shooting pictures when it's cold out. I haven't been garage saling since before the holidays, but in Spalding there's this weird tradition of continuing garage sales throughout winter— people just move them into their actual garages. It's still cold, but the snow has melted on most people's driveways and it's super sunny, which isn't ideal for shooting but it's great for walking around.

The first garage has bins and bins of baby toys and racks of kids clothes on one side, and on the other are long tables set up with old-fashioned record players, and those plastic milk crates filled with records. In the middle are knick-knacks, mismatched teacups, silverware and glasses. It's pretty much the standard garage-sale fare, a little bit of everything. Feels like my photography right now. I still haven't found my focus. I thought it was going to be portraits, but since Tisch I've found so much I like about shooting inanimate objects. The stories they hold are too intriguing. But it doesn't mean I don't like shooting people too. One of the instructors at Tisch said finding your niche is like having a feeling. You can't overanalyze it, you just keep shooting random stuff until you get that feeling—your calling. The thing you want to shoot above all else.

"You in the market for baby stuff?" a woman says. Her hair's blonde, with streaks of gray. I realize I've been hovering over the land of stuffed animals. "A little sister or brother on the way?"

I shake my head and smile. "Uh, no. Just looking around."

"Our daughter's done having kids; the youngest is seven. And they moved to Texas. We only see them once a year and they're past all this stuff. No more grandkids on the way." There's wistfulness in her eyes. Her husband comes and puts an arm around her.

I think about Mom, how she only has me, and when I leave for New York (hopefully) in a year and a half, how she's going to be alone. Is she going to sell all my stuff? Is she going to cry to strangers? But what can I do to help her? I can't exactly have babies just so she has grandkids—I've seen *Teen Mom*, no thank you. And I don't want to stay home just so that she isn't lonely. I spy a bunch of books tucked behind a rocking chair. "Do you have a copy of *Catcher in the Rye*?" I ask, and the guy scratches his chin.

"I thought I was the only crazy one up this early on a Sunday morning," a voice says behind me.

I turn and see Ben standing by a crate of records.

"Hey," I say.

"What are you doing here?" he asks.

"It's kind of my thing." I hold up my camera. "What are *you* doing here?"

"My mom's birthday's coming up and I was awake anyway. My little brothers wake up at like 6 a.m., so there's no sleeping in even if you want to."

"You have brothers?"

"Yeah, well, half-brothers. Alex and Aidan. Anyway, I'm on the hunt for a cool album for her. I know I could just look online but I figured this was as easy and it's actually more peaceful than being forced to watch another episode of *SpongeBob*."

I realize then that I'm on his street, a few doors down from his house.

"You have fun last night?" he asks, rifling through the albums.

"Yeah." I say. "So Gemma, huh?"

He shrugs but doesn't say anything, instead keeps sorting through the albums. He pulls off his wool hat and I notice the word BOB embroidered on the back.

"Who's Bob?" I say, thinking he's going to say the hat was his grandpa's or something.

"Oh, my initials. Benjamin Owen Baxter. My mom's super into monogramming. You should see our front hall closet. It's like an L.L.Bean showroom."

"So, can I call you Bob?"

With Gemma on the horizon, I already feel less pressure to make sure Ben doesn't think there's anything between us. It's like I can be myself again.

"Please don't."

"I'm calling you Bob." I grin.

"What's *your* middle name?"

"Isabelle."

I can see him working it out in his head. "*PIG*? Your initials are *PIG* and you're making fun of *BOB*? *Oh Wilbur . . .*" He tosses his hat at me. I flip it over in my hands, thinking.

I've always wondered why Mom and Dad clearly

didn't consider my initials when naming me, but it dawns on me now, my initials weren't meant to be PIG. Mom was with David: I was meant to be PIW.

"Are you OK?" Ben asks. I hand him his hat.

"I just thought of something. My initials. They should've been PIW."

"Whoa." Neither of us says anything for a moment.

"Hey, how about you call me Ben and I call you Pippa and we forget we ever had this conversation?"

I half-smile. "Deal. So. Your mom's into records?"

Ben flips through the crate of albums from the '70s. "My mom has a vintage wood Crosley. She got me a NAD 533 for my birthday last year. Are you into records?"

I shake my head. "Not really. I'm quite happy with the modern technology of iTunes."

He laughs and nods at the milk crates. "I'll show you the difference the NADINATOR makes sometime." He adds another LP to the pile he's accumulated on the table beside the crate. "Hey, what are you doing after this? Want to shoot some photos for the alumni mural?"

"I'm not sure. I was . . . probably going to hang out with Dylan," I say even though he still hasn't texted me back yet, which probably means he's still sleeping. His parents will be home by tonight. If we're going to do it, we're losing our opportunity. I wonder if he's mad that I didn't come over last night. Or leave the party with him. What's his deal anyway?

"You know," I say, changing my mind. "I'm actually free right now."

"Great. Are you hungry? I'm hungry. We could eat somewhere Spalding kids eat," Ben says. I nod. "Let me just pay for these." He hands the woman a few dollars and then we head down the driveway. "Wanna just go back to my place, I can dump this stuff off and we can grab my car?"

"Sure." We turn left and walk a few houses up the street to Ben's.

"How about the Orange Turtle? A bunch of alumni listed it on the Facebook page as their favorite spot," he suggests as we get into his car.

Thoughts go to Dylan and our last breakfast together there. I'd kind of pictured us there again this morning, eating pancakes after our farewell-Virginia sleepover.

"It's an institution," I say. "Tradition dictates that everyone meets there morning after senior prom. It's been happening forever. Even my mom and her friends did it," I say, buckling my seatbelt. He starts the car and turns on the radio. "But we should text Gemma too, so she doesn't feel left out."

"Yeah, sure," Ben says. "You want to text her?"

She says she's still in her pajamas but to go ahead without her and she'll catch up to us in an hour or so. Ben pulls into the parking lot and we walk inside. The smell of greasy bacon and pancakes fills the air. The diner is only half full. It's in that limbo morning time: later than the early birds but too early for late-morning brunch types. I purposely avert my gaze from the far corner—where Dylan and I always sit—and grab the first booth by the door. I slide into the red vinyl seat across from

Ben. A waitress wearing a white apron over a red gingham dress, her hair in a bun, comes over and hands us two worn, plastic menus. "Coffees?"

"Sure," Ben says, then nods to me. "Can you put chocolate syrup in hers?"

The waitress pours coffee in both our mugs and then grabs some creamers from her apron pocket and places them on the table. "I'll see what I can do."

"You're still doing that I assume?" Ben says, adding milk to his coffee. "What's wrong?" he asks and I realize I've just let out a big sigh. It's not that Ben remembers my whole "chocolate syrup in coffee actually makes it drinkable" experiment from New York, which is something David introduced me to. It's that Dylan doesn't even know that. I came here with Dylan last Saturday, but when the waitress went to pour coffee in our mugs, instead of me asking for chocolate syrup and telling Dylan about it—or seeing whether he wanted to try it too—Dylan just told her we didn't drink coffee and would have water instead. And I went along with it, because I liked the idea that we had that in common—Dylan and me, McCutter and Greene, we don't drink coffee like everyone else. It was stupid, but it was a little thing I wanted to preserve, even if it wasn't true anymore.

"I don't think I can talk about this with you. It's weird," I say.

"Dylan stuff? I can give you the guy perspective—if you want."

I grab a white sugar packet from the small square metal container.

"Dace says girls and guys can't be friends. It's the law of attraction."

"What are you saying—you're attracted to me?"

"No. I'm not! But I think you're . . ." My face reddens. "Nevermind." The sugar packet becomes fascinating.

"You think I'm into you," he says matter of factly, then sips his coffee.

"No. I know you're not. Anymore. You're into Gemma."

"Exactly. Gemma." He folds his hands on his lap as the waitress returns with a stainless steel creamer filled with chocolate syrup.

"Go nuts, sweetheart. You two ready to order?" I order the #1 special and Ben says he'll have the waffles, and the waitress takes our menus and shoves them in the front pocket of her apron.

Ben leans forward. "We're going to the dance together." He smiles.

"Oh, great," I say, acting relieved. But I also feel something else. Dylan and I really haven't even talked about the dance since he shrugged off the band thing. Of course we'll go together, he's my boyfriend. He doesn't have to ask me. And it's not like I really asked him. Huh.

"Dylan was in a band, right?" Ben asks, as though reading my mind. "Are they playing at the dance?"

"Yeah, Rules for Breaking the Rules. But I'm not sure. He's . . ." My sighs are uncontrollable.

"Come on. You're killing me. Spill it. Pretend I'm Dace. Wait, better yet, pretend I'm Dr. Judy." He clears his throat. "Tell me how things are going with Dylan."

I laugh nervously.

"Is this funny to you?" he says, in the exact way Dr. Judy asks questions. While we were at Tisch, Ben and I discovered we both go to see the same therapist, Dr. Judy. Ben, because of his dad, stepdad, mom, moving issues and rebellious ways, and me, because of Dad dying mostly, and the ensuing panic attacks. She helped a lot, and aside from one check-in over the Christmas break, I've been pretty much Judy-free for a few months.

"We're just *off*. I feel out of sync with him and . . . I don't know, he seems sort of distant. And there's this girl, Muse. Who I was jealous of, but then I found out she had a boyfriend, but then I think she just broke up with her boyfriend and . . ."

"Hmm," Ben says. "Wait, what's Dylan doing this year anyway?"

"Well, that's the thing. Nothing really."

"Is he doing a gap year?"

"Kind of," I say.

"Maybe that's it," he says. "Maybe he's trying to figure next year out or something and it has nothing to do with you or this Muse girl. Or maybe it has everything to do with you. Like maybe he's thinking about where to go next year and how that's going to work with you."

"Yeah, maybe," I say unconvincingly. "Of course, selfishly I wish he'd stay here, but he can't have another year like this year, just hanging out. And he deferred Harvard, so I assume he'll go . . ."

"Dude got into Harvard?" Ben watches me. I look down at his hands.

"Well . . . yeah."

"So why'd he defer?"

I bite my lip. "Long story."

"Come on. I can't help you if you don't give me all the information."

I'm not sure if he's being Dr. Judy or Ben, but I shake my head.

"Come on, Pippa. I'm your *friend*."

The waitress brings us our food. I take out my camera, then focus in on my plate, and snap a few pics. "Wait," I say. "Don't eat yet. Your plate may come out better than mine." He puts his fork down and leans back in his chair as I snap away. I pull the camera away from my face and check the results. "Not bad." I put my camera down on the seat beside me and wave my hand. "OK, you may now waffle it up." I stab a pancake with my fork then cut it into bite-sized pieces.

"Come on. Spill it sister," he says while pouring syrup on his waffles.

I bite my lip and look around. "Well . . . you can't tell anyone. He would kill me if he knew you knew. Or anybody knew." I put my fork down. "But the reason he's still here, and not at school—he had non-Hodgkin's lymphoma." I pause. "Cancer." Ben's eyes widen slightly, but then he regains composure. "He's fine now, but I still worry about it. Like, what if he's not?"

Ben's silent for a moment. "Whoa."

"I know." I take a sip of water.

"You know what? I think you cut the guy some slack. That's a lot to deal with. And he loves you.

That's for sure. Give him some time. If something's wrong, he'll tell you. Otherwise, just go about things as if they're normal."

It's not like Ben's said anything profound, but it sticks. He's right. I just have to assume everything's fine. Great. I pull out my notebook and we start brainstorming for the alumni project. Before I know it, the waitress comes back to clear our plates. "You hardly touched yours," she says to me, then asks if I want it to go.

"Sure," I say, then stand. "I'm going to get some shots of the décor." Wanting a few options for the mural, I snap some pics of the counter, the soda machines, the tile backsplash behind the grill then return to our booth just as Gemma walks through the front doors. She looks cute, in a matching gray wool cap and mitts, which she pulls off, waving to us and hurrying over.

"Hey guys," she says and slides into the booth beside Ben. He puts his arm around her and kisses her on the cheek.

"Hey yourself."

They seem happy. Ben's right. I need to just act like nothing's wrong. If Dylan hasn't told me differently, then we're good. "Do you mind if I go?" I say. "I think I'll head over to Dylan's. Bring him the rest of my breakfast." I hold up the takeout box. "See you two at school tomorrow."

CHAPTER 11

There's no answer when I knock on Dylan's front door, and he doesn't answer his phone, so I figure he must still be asleep, even though it's creeping up on noon. Despite having the key I've never actually used it—either Dylan or one of his parents have always been there when I've popped over unexpectedly—but this time, the door's locked so I use the key to surprise him with breakfast in bed, even if it is my leftovers.

Dylan's boots are kicked off inside the front door, and in the kitchen there's an empty pizza box and a bunch of beer bottles. But the house is quiet. I head up to his room but find it empty. Messy, but empty. And it smells different—that familiar mix of boy and Eau Savage, his cologne, is replaced with . . . incense? Since when does Dylan do incense?

I scan the room for other clues, but come up

short. I place the takeout breakfast on his desk and sit down on the edge of his bed, thinking back to the first time Dylan brought me here. When we first kissed on his bed, when we first laid side by side, our bodies touching. How we fell asleep and woke up with just enough time to scramble to get me home before my curfew.

Voices downstairs interrupt my thoughts. I stand, suddenly nervous. What if it's his parents, home early, and I'm here in his room, alone with a box of cold pancakes? Too weird for words? But the sound of Dylan's familiar laugh erases that thought. It's him, and . . . a girl? Callie, maybe? I don't have time to figure it out before their voices get closer: Dylan's coming down the hallway, toward his room. Behind him is the girl. Muse. They're laughing and completely oblivious that I'm watching them for a good three seconds. And then they both see me. Muse stops laughing, but doesn't stop smiling. She looks at Dylan, whose face turns red. He coughs and regains composure.

"What are you doing here?"

I expected those words, in some form, I suppose, but not like that. Like, *Wow, you're here, I'm so happy to see you.* Not the tone he has.

It is *not good.*

This is where Muse should say, "I should go." Has she never watched a romantic comedy with an easily avoidable mixup? She should leave and Dylan will tell me there's nothing to worry about, that they ran into each other and Muse wanted help buying a gift to win back her boyfriend and Dylan was giving her something—something music related he knows

Patrick will like? But instead . . . I realize I have just been standing here dumbstruck.

Muse looks from Dylan to me and back to him. "Do you want me to go?"

Yes! I plead on the inside. Why is Dylan hesitating? He looks like he's actually trying to decide. "I didn't know you were coming over," he says. To me. I'm stunned. Is he actually saying that I, his girlfriend, can't surprise him?

"I texted you," I say, lamely. "I . . ."

"Muse and I made plans to jam," he says. "Did you know Muse writes her own songs?"

Nope. I did not know that.

"Oh." It's all I can think of to say. And I keep standing there, just willing him to say something like, "But we'll do it another time." Or "Muse, I think you should go." Or, "Maybe we can all hang out together." But he doesn't say anything. He just stands there too.

The moment feels unreal and seems to last an eternity. It's nothing Dylan's saying or not saying, it's just something in the air that feels off. Like I know what's going on without wanting to know. I can't react properly: I don't know whether to grab my stuff and go, or sit down on the bed like this is all fine and invite myself to their "jam session." Everything is getting fuzzy, hazy, I feel both hot and cold at once, and a second later, I'm pushing my way to the door, racing down the stairs. As I'm cramming my feet into my boots, I hear Dylan.

"Sorry about that." He sounds embarrassed. I look up, but he's not on the stairs apologizing to *me*. He's still in his room. He's saying those words to Muse. I grab my coat and rush outside without putting it on.

● ● ●

Dylan doesn't call, not while I'm crying on the phone to Dace, and not after we've finally hung up what seems like hours later. I lie on my bed, staring at the ceiling, checking my phone every few minutes, which only makes the time pass even more slowly. I rearrange my room, then remember why it's been the same layout for years—it's the only way all the furniture actually fits—and put everything back. I try to cull my photos for this week's photo club theme: bokeh, a.k.a., blur in photo speak. But my eyes are too blurry, my head too fuzzy to focus. I sit at the table through a dinner I don't want to eat, and then retreat back to my room, shunning Mom's offer to watch a movie together. I try to sleep, but my mind won't let me. I try to stay awake but my eyelids get too heavy. Every time I relive the moment, I feel hurt, embarrassment, anger. In the middle of the night, I turn my light on and grab the picture of Dad, the one where he's standing outside what's now Emmy's apartment in New York. The one that I keep on my nightstand.

He just stares back at me, waiting for me to figure this out on my own, just like he always does. He never has the answers. Because he's gone, and it's just me and I can't talk to Mom. The picture goes blurry beyond my tears.

Eventually I fall back to sleep.

CHAPTER 12

Dylan: Pickup alert! Need a ride home?

Seriously? Photo club is just ending, and even though I've been checking my phone every five seconds all day, and a text from Dylan is *exactly* what I wanted, I'm annoyed. Like, really? I'm supposed to act like nothing happened? I take five deep breaths—but quick ones—and then reply simply.

Me: Sure.

I make my way as slowly as I can possibly bear to, which is not much slower than a jog, to the parking lot, where his car is parked in one of the front spots. I pause for a moment, trying to compose myself, and consider what I'll say to him. I want to be mad at him—but I don't want to ruin the fact that he's picked me up, and that, maybe, things are fine between us. But I also don't want to act as though nothing's wrong at all—and let him think that he has all the control in our relationship. That he can treat me the way he treated me yesterday, and I'll just go along with it. "See you tomorrow, Pip," Gemma says as she and Ben pass me and head toward Ben's car. I take a deep breath, walk over and open the passenger side door.

"Hey," he says, as I get in, leaning over to kiss me.

I give a half-smile as we pull apart, then stash my bag at my feet and pull my seatbelt across my body.

"Want to get something to eat?" he asks.

"Um, sure?" I say, totally confused. He takes a left onto Winchester and then a right onto Haven and I realize he's headed to Scoops. The first time Dylan tried to take me here, I passed out, but a lot of therapy and a lot of Dylan have made Scoops a normal place again, which is a good thing because they added burgers and caramel milkshakes to their menu.

Scoops is packed with kids from Spalding mostly, with a long lineup at the counter. The music's always loud, but that, combined with animated chatter and the clatter of metal spoons on glass sundae bowls means Dylan has to shout at the hostess to tell her there's two of us. She leads us over to a table by the window, and I spot Ben and Gemma sitting across from each other at a table on the other side of the place. "Caramel sundae, no nuts?" he asks and I nod and put my coat on the back of my chair as Dylan heads up to the counter to order. Ben's heading over at the same time, and he nods to me, then gets in line behind Dylan. I go over to talk to Gemma, even though we just saw each other 10 minutes ago.

"I have to pee, come to the bathroom with me?" she asks and I follow her down the hall at the back of the restaurant.

"Everything OK? You seem bummed out today," she says from the stall.

"Yeah," I say, hopping up on the counter. A second later my phone buzzes and I pull it out of my pocket.

Ben: Ugh SORRY.

I hold my phone out to Gemma as she comes out of the stall. "Any idea what he's talking about?"

She shrugs, washing her hands. "No clue." She applies a bit of lipgloss and fixes her hair then turns to me. I'm still staring at my phone.

"You ready?" She holds open the door and I follow her out of the bathroom. Dylan's back at our booth and I slide in across from him.

"What's wrong?" I ask, noticing the look on his face.

He stares at me, his green eyes steely. "You told *Ben*?"

"Told Ben what?" I say, my heart pounding.

"About me?" he whispers. "After I told you I didn't want anyone to know . . . You told Ben Fucking Baxter?"

My face is burning. "What did he say?" I pull at the hem of my sweater. My stomach's in knots.

"Nothing. He didn't have to say anything. He gave

me That Look. That Head Tilted Sympathy Look that said it all."

"He . . . I . . . he was giving me advice."

"*Ben* was? What could he possibly be giving you advice about that required you telling him the one thing you knew I don't want anyone knowing? How to date a recovering cancer patient?"

I sit back, digging my shoulder blades into the metal frame of the chair. "No. We were just *talking*. Why are you so upset?"

His eyes are cold. "I'm upset because you broke my confidence. Since when are you and Ben even talking?"

"Since Tisch. It was kind of hard to avoid him—it would've been impossible to avoid anyone."

"Well, I don't see you talking to anyone else from Tisch."

I roll my eyes, exasperated. "Ben's in photo club, we're working on this mural for the alumni project together . . ." I shrug. "I guess he's become a friend. But it's totally platonic."

He rolls his eyes. "There's no way he's not still into you."

"You're being ridiculous," I say. "I'm sorry I told him your big bad secret, but I needed someone to talk to."

He shakes his head. "Then talk to me. Or Dace. Why him? Are *you* still into him?"

"No! I just didn't tell you we were friends because I didn't want you to get jealous when there's no reason to be. But why are we even talking about this? I thought you were bringing me here to apologize about yesterday." I throw up my hands. "Forget Ben—what about you *dismissing* me to hang out with Muse?" I lean in and lower my voice. "Do you know how horrible you made me feel?"

I hope he'll say that it's different, that even though, yes, Muse and Patrick broke up, she's heartbroken and wanted advice on how to win him back. That they'd been together forever, and she needed a friend to talk to, someone that could see both sides, since he's friends with both of them. That there's absolutely no attraction there, but of course, he doesn't say any of that.

"Because I didn't drop my plans for you?"

I'm stunned. "It was just the . . . way you handled it. You gave me a key, and then basically implied I wasn't welcome to use it."

"Muse felt really awkward."

"It was only awkward because you didn't tell Muse to leave."

"I didn't feel comfortable asking her to leave. I'd asked her to come over. We were going to jam together. And she lives an hour away, and you and I—we didn't have any plans. And we don't have that kind of relationship. At least, I didn't think we did."

"What kind?"

"The jealous kind. Or the kind where I insist you drop all other plans for me, and vice versa." He has a point. I'm about to give in, but then he keeps talking. "I don't go barging into your photo club meetings. When you wanted to join ski club, I encouraged you to."

"But I didn't join."

"But you could have. That was your choice. Yesterday felt like an invasion of my free time." The look on his face—it's a mix of exasperation and frustration—hits me right in the gut. Anger, that I could handle, but there's something about his look that hurts in all the worst places. I'm annoying him.

"Fine, I get it," I say defensively. The waitress arrives with our ice cream. As she glances from Dylan to me, she looks like she wants to be anywhere other than standing in front of us, and I look down to avoid eye contact as she puts our bowls down. The whole diner suddenly seems quiet even though it's noisy as ever.

"Can we just forget about this?" Dylan stabs his sundae with his spoon.

"What if it happens again?"

"We'll cross that bridge when we get to it."

"I need *some* kind of resolution on this. So you're just going to keep hanging out with Muse—"

"Yeah. Just like you hang out with Ben." He lets out a frustrated sigh and pushes his bowl away. "It's probably good we're finally fighting. It's been feeling like this for a while."

"Like what?"

"Like I can't do my own thing. You have your own life, and you expect me to just fit into it. Picking you up after school, going to parties, the dance . . . I'm not in high school anymore, Pippa."

"I thought you liked picking me up after school," I say, my voice shaking. "If you don't want to do something, you could just tell me. You don't have to . . ."

He shakes his head. "But you want to do all these things I don't want to do, with people I don't want to see anymore. I finished that part of my life, and I want to move on from it."

"Then move on! Party at Roxy's with all your cool band friends every night. Don't come to another lame high school party. And the dance? Everyone who ever went to Spalding will be there. But fine, don't go. I'll go by myself."

"It's not . . . it's not *what* I want to do. It's *why* I want to do it. Do you get what I mean?"

"No."

We both sit there, neither of us touching our ice cream, which is starting to melt in its bowls.

"Wanna go?" he asks.

"Yes," I say, standing forcefully, grabbing my coat and bag, not bothering to put them on as I rush through the restaurant, tears stinging my eyes. I look around when I get outside, trying to remember where Dylan parked. The cold burns my watery eyes. Dylan brushes past me, nodding to the car at the far end of the row. He opens my door and I get in and then he goes around to his side and gets into the driver's seat. A minute later we're back on the road, driving home in silence. I play over the conversation in my head, trying to think of what to say at this point. Eventually we pull into my driveway. He switches off the ignition and then turns to me.

"Pippa, it's this: for six months I was sick. It was all I was. I hid from anyone who didn't know. And then we got together, and it was great, but I realize now that I was kind of just hiding out in your life, playing the boyfriend. But those two weeks working for the Cherry Blasters, I wasn't 'cancer teen,' I wasn't 'Pippa's boyfriend.' I was Dylan. I got to get a glimpse of a life that I've wanted so bad—being on the road with a band. And it was liberating. God, it was so liberating."

I don't know how to take what he's saying. So I just nod.

"Hanging around the high school scene, doing stuff with people that knew me last year, it's just a reminder of who I was. The old me. The guy who got cancer and put off Harvard."

I feel defensive. "I'm not trying to hold you back. I'm fine with you being New Dylan, or whatever."

"But I don't think you are. You're disappointed I won't go to the dance. You zone out whenever I talk about my time on the road."

I let out a deep breath and my shoulders slump. "Of course I'm disappointed. You're my boyfriend, and it's on Valentine's Day, and it would be the first dance I ever went to with a date I actually loved, and you could play with your band—"

"That's the thing. Sounds great for you, but for me that means coming back as the guy who's just hanging around Spalding, doing *nothing* this year, while everyone else is off at college. You don't know how that feels."

I can feel tears welling up. "I guess, no I don't. So what—you want to spend more time with those guys? With Muse?"

"This isn't about Muse."

"Then . . . you just don't want anything to do with

your past or anyone in it. That's what you're saying."
I swallow the lump in my throat. "What about prom next year? Or a New Year's party, or my birthday party?" I know I'm getting ahead of myself, but it feels overwhelming. "This doesn't seem fair to me, Dylan. Like you're making all these rules, and I don't know how I fit into them."

"Yeah," he says.

"Yeah what?" And then I get it. "Is this because I know you had cancer?"

He pauses, maybe a second too long. "You used to be the girl who didn't know. I was just Dylan to you. And it was so great. Now you're, like, Cancer Mom. You come with me to my appointments. You ask me if I got the results. And you nag me about drinking."

"I just . . . didn't think you were drinking. I wasn't nagging you." My hands are shaking.

"What does it matter anyway? Every other normal guy my age drinks. You drink."

"You're right. Fine! It doesn't matter. I'm not judging you, I'm just asking." My voice wavers. "Because I care, Dylan. Aren't I allowed to care? You may recall that the last person I loved who had cancer died."

Dylan stares at me, but like he's looking through me, not at me. Then he sighs and rubs his face with his hands. "I'm sorry—of course you care. And I'm sorry if I remind you of losing your dad. That must really suck." He fiddles with the steering wheel. "But every time you ask me something like that it makes me think of being sick and scared. And I . . . I just don't want to have to be reminded of that."

Tears stream down my face. Time passes. I don't know how much, but it feels like neither of us knows what's left to say.

"I think we should break up."

The words come from me.

"Are you serious?" Dylan looks genuinely stunned.

"Yes." I swipe at my tears and put on the strongest face I have. "I don't see how there's room for me in your new life, now that I know how you feel. I don't want to compromise who I am. Or how I act. And neither do you, that much is clear."

I want him to say that we'll find a way, that I mean too much to him. He looks at me intently and I look away because I know if I keep looking at his eyes, I'll break down. When I look back up, his expression has hardened. "Yeah, OK, if that's what you want."

I sit for a moment, hoping he'll say something else, but his hand is on the keys in the ignition, and he's staring straight ahead. I grab my bag off the floor and open the door, then get out, realizing this may be the last time I'll ever be getting out of Dylan's car. I close the door for the last time, and walk up the driveway, refusing to look back.

CHAPTER 13

Everything reminds me of him. My English notebook where I've doodled DM+PG inside hearts. The mug with my name on it that he gave me, filled with Twizzlers, for Christmas. The ticket stub from the Cherry Blasters concert pinned to my bulletin board. The random business card we found in the gazebo at Hannover Park for Harry Combs, barber. Notes he'd slip in my school bag when I wasn't looking. My entire Instagram account, mostly because every photo reminds me of him in some way. The staircase to the basement makes me think of the night Dylan jumped up, landed on the banister and slid the rest of the way down, all without spilling the glass of Coke he was holding. There's a water-stain ring on the kitchen table that reminds me of Wednesday nights when he'd come for dinner with Mom and me.

I've never broken up with someone before, but I always imagined if I did, it would be liberating, that it would be because I was no longer in love with him, and I would be happy to not ever have to see or talk to or think about him again. This is the exact opposite of that. I miss him and all the little things about him.

On Tuesday I go to school but only because Mom forces me. I give my Streeters column to Jeffrey to complete for the following week's *Hall Pass*. On Wednesday I scroll through every single one of Muse's hundreds of Instagram photos. On Thursday I check her page about 23 times for updates. On Friday she posts a picture of her and Dylan: he's holding his guitar, and she's got a notebook on her lap—her head touching his as they lean together to fit in the frame. My heart beats faster and my eyes sting. My hands shake as I close the app and toss my phone aside, then flop back on my pillow, staring at the ceiling.

I try to analyze what I'm feeling, Dr. Judy style. Am I jealous? Or sad? Or mad? I decide it's All of the Above. Are they *together*? Is it because I broke up with Dylan? Or would they have gotten together no matter what, and it was only a matter of time until he broke up with me? Or did Dylan cheat on me? I text Dace but she doesn't respond, which is weird because she's basically been checking in with me every five seconds since Dylan and I broke up. Emma and Gemma are also MIA, and then I remember they're all at ski club. I go to bed at 7 and don't get up until 11 on Saturday morning. Mom has breakfast waiting on the kitchen table and an appointment scheduled with Dr. Judy.

• • •

Dace arrives on the doorstep for Sleepover Saturday laden with two huge beach bags—one filled with her sleepover stuff and the other fully stocked with break-up survival snacks: chips, Cokes and a bag she's filled at the bulk candy store with every type of candy, except the one I eat every Sleepover Saturday: Twizzlers.

"Nice try," I say half-heartedly.

"At what?"

"Trying to make me forget my usual."

She shakes her head. "Moving on."

We settle into my room, pillows and blankets in a cozy nest on the floor. Then she busts a *Cosmo* out of her bag and flips it open, pointing at a small article in the corner.

"What?" I peer at the page.

"It says it takes a quarter of the time you dated someone to get over them. No matter whether you were the dumper or the dumpee."

I do the math: Dylan and I were officially together for 14 weeks but I always cheat and count from two weeks earlier—the day I first saw him at St. Christopher's and my crush on him became something much, much more. So that means four solid weeks to get over him. Six days down, three weeks and a day to go. I look at the calendar on my phone and count it out.

"Oh god, my get-over-him day is *Valentine's Day*. That's just cruel. I don't think I can do it. I've worn the same jeans to school all week. I haven't washed my hair since Wednesday."

"Both are good for you. The jeans are setting and your hair is creating natural oils to clean itself." Dace props up my laptop so we can both see it and then loads Netflix. "But you're going to need to eat a lot of this candy."

I start to cry.

CHAPTER 14: THREE WEEKS UNTIL I'M OVER HIM

I haven't been in the darkroom, Dad's darkroom, since before Dad died. I tried the door once, right after he died. It was locked, and I took it as a sign. Mom has the key, somewhere, but she hasn't been in there either. As though she also can't bear to deal with the one room that was all Dad's.

Mom's sitting at the little desk she has in the kitchen, sorting through bills. Her laptop is flipped open and she's staring intently at the screen.

"I need to go into the darkroom."

She looks up and shuts her laptop. "Are you sure?"

I nod, but then my face crumples into the human equivalent of a Shar-Pei. I blink away the tears. "Mom, I just really need to be in the darkroom right now."

"OK." She opens the drawer where she keeps

rubber bands, Scotch tape, sticky notes and other sundries. She hands me the key. "I love you, sweetie."

Dad's darkroom used to be the fruit cellar, back when my grandparents lived here. It was their house—the house Mom grew up in. They moved here when she was four and Emmy was two, and then Mom moved to New York, and Emmy later, and then when Mom got pregnant with me she moved back home, and Dad came with her. Grandma and Grandpa moved into an apartment a few years later to give us more space.

At first, Dad worked at a portrait studio with another photographer, but after a few years he decided to go out on his own. He never had a studio in town, he just worked from home, which he said he liked because he was always here when I got home from school. Mom was usually home too, because she didn't work, though she used to teach yoga once in a while.

The darkroom is down a hallway at the bottom of the basement stairs, with a heavy wooden door and a wrought-iron handle. Grandma used to store her preserves in it, even after they moved. She had shelves upon shelves of jam made from every possible fruit. She'd start every year with strawberry, then make strawberry rhubarb, then apricot, then peach, then peach melba, which is a combination of peaches and raspberries, then raspberry on its own and finally blueberry. In the fall she'd move on to pickling vegetables: beets and cauliflower, carrots and mini onions, sweet pickles and dill pickles. The cellar was full when Grandma died. From then on,

Mom was strict about finishing a jar of jam before opening another. To make it last. One day, we realized we only had one jar left. It was Dad who came up with the idea of having the Jam session to make what would've otherwise been a sad occasion into a memorable, fun one. He made posters for it and plastered them around the house. The party started at 8 p.m. with directions on how to get to the cellar from, say, the second floor bathroom. Dad only played music by the Jam, this band from the '70s. I invited Dace, and we danced and ate jam on crackers. Dad took pictures. There's this great photo of the three of us—Dad, Mom and me—that Dace took, each holding up a cracker with jam, Dad holding the final jar. The pic is a bit blurry—Dace was laughing when she took it—but we're all laughing too, and the way the strobe lights are hitting us, we're a rainbow of color.

I unlock the door and take a deep breath, then turn the wrought-iron handle. The familiar smell of developing chemicals hits me and it's so much a part of my memory of Dad, it's like smelling his deodorant or his aftershave. I pull on the string that's dangling from above and the bare bulb casts a yellow light on the room. The metal developing basins are in front of me. Overhead, photos are clothespinned along a long piece of string stretching from one wall to the other.

I dust off the old recliner in the corner. The creamy white leather is soft and worn and I sink into it like it's made of marshmallows. Sometimes Dad would work down here so late that he would fall asleep in the chair and Mom would have to wake him up in the morning. She'd make coffee and then ask me to bring it down to him. I'd hold a red dish towel under the cup to absorb any spills as I navigated the stairs down to the basement.

I pull the lever on the side and let my body stretch out. Cobwebs dangle from the wood beams and pipes on the ceiling. Dad's old wood desk looks frozen in time: a pile of invoices sits under a paperweight—a pet rock I painted when I was in preschool. The mug I gave him one Father's Day—which used to say *I ♥ Dad*, but the words erased, and all that's left is the heart—holds a stash of pens. The yellow wrapping on a roll of Kodak Ektachrome film catches my eye. I grab the roll and press it between my palms. It takes me 10 minutes to prep the developing station and then I'm extracting the film from the canister. I've got to see what's on the roll—I need something from Dad, some message from beyond to get me through this. In the movies, I'd find one last roll and there'd be a photo in there. Something I'd never seen before. Something to connect me to Dad and give me some moment of peace and clarity. But 20 minutes pass and the photos turn out to be . . . well, of some sort of squash? Close-ups of yams. The odd pumpkin. Maybe Dad was working on a project about harvest vegetables at some point and forgot to develop the roll? The framing is classic Evan Greene, but the images have nothing at all to say about my strange, so-called life.

Hours have passed by the time I come out of the darkroom. After finding and developing two more rolls, I've inspected every single frame, and that gives me an odd sense of completion, of knowing that there's nothing left uncovered, but I can't help feeling disheartened and empty. Vulnerable. The main floor is quiet, but the distinct smell of paint hits me as I walk down the front hall, toward the stairs to the second floor.

"Pippa?" Mom calls from upstairs. I follow the scent and find Mom standing on a stepladder, her jean overalls, (formerly) white T-shirt and arms all splattered with peach paint.

"What are you doing?" I say. But it's obvious. All the furniture's in the middle of the room, covered in drop sheets. The green—the forest green the walls have been forever—is gone. The walls have been primed white, and Mom's working on the wall her bed is usually up against. It's peach.

She looks down at me. "No bedroom should be green. It feels like a massive empty field. Nothing as far as the eye can see. It was depressing."

I want to point out that probably what's depressing about her bedroom is that her husband is dead and now she sleeps alone, but instead I state the obvious. "So you're painting it peach?"

Mom looks around the room from the top of the ladder. "Time for a change. Want to help?"

"Are you kidding?"

Mom looks surprised.

"Dad *hated* the color peach," I point out. "Or have you already forgotten?"

I practically spit the words. Mom stares at me, shocked. She climbs down from her ladder, puts her paintbrush on top of the paint can, then grabs a sheet from a pile on the floor and puts it on the bed. "Sit."

I shake my head no.

"What's going on with you, Pippa?"

"*What's going on*? Why are you doing this?"

"The peach or the room?" She doesn't wait for an answer. "Your father may have hated peach, but that's not *why* I'm painting it peach."

"Oh really?" I say.

"I've always hated this green. For years. Your father was well aware I wanted to change it. And we had the peach in the basement. I just need a change. This was easy, and free."

"So you can forget all about him?"

She winces. "Pippa. Stop. This has nothing to do with forgetting your father. It has to do with me. It's cathartic. It's *symbolic*. I read that it's a stage I need to go through."

"So that's it?! Forget everything you loved about Dad, forget the good times, forget that what you shared was special. Forget that you told him you loved him, that you'd love him forever? You're not willing to fight for him, fight for what you had? You just reach a bump in the road and you're just so eager to take a new path? How can you do that? How can you have cared so much, and then just like that, you don't care at all?" I kick at the drop sheets and they sort of puff up into the air and I grab at them with my hands, and then throw them back on the ground.

"Pippa!" Mom says, alarmed. "What are you talking about? What's gotten into you? Fight for what? Your father's gone. How can I fight for someone who isn't here? Pippa? Pippa?" She's still talking, but I can't hear her, the words are a blur and

I realize I'm bawling. And then, a second later, her arms are around me, hugging me tight.

"It's not fair, Mom. It's just not fair. I love Dylan so much. Why doesn't he fight for me?"

I can't get any more words out, I can't catch my breath I'm crying so hard. Mom rocks me in her arms, pulling me into her so that I feel weightless, whispering in my ear, "It's OK, honey, it's OK."

CHAPTER 15: TWO AND A HALF WEEKS UNTIL I'M OVER HIM

I don't know what I'm looking for. I open the drawers of Dad's desk, move books, check his filing cabinet. There has to be something. A clue. An answer. And then, on a Thursday afternoon when I've skipped a *Hall Pass* meeting to instead come home and be alone, I pull open the bottom drawer of the filing cabinet, something I'm sure I've done a dozen times already, but this time, I lift up all the papers—receipts, notes and who knows what else—and underneath is a photo, 4x6, color, matte finish. A picture of Dace and me: we're skating on the pond, being totally ridiculous, carefree. It was only last winter, but it seems so long ago. I lift the picture to look more closely, and underneath is another. My mom and me washing her beat-up Honda, suds on both our faces thanks to the impromptu water fight she started. Under that one is another. And another.

Shots that he'd developed from film, but which never got scanned for the photo album Dad created at the end of each year. "One for the yearbook," he'd say whenever he captured something memorable— a birthday, something funny, whatever.

These are the pictures that didn't quite work out. Underdeveloped. Slightly out of focus. A blur of movement. But they're real. They're life.

And then I realize that we don't have a yearbook for this past year, for the first time since I was born. I think over last year: the trip we took to Disney World on my school break in March. Mother's Day, when we surprised Mom by making her stay in bed for the entire day, which was what she'd been saying for years was all she really wanted. Then Dad got sick. What would the rest of the year show? Him in the hospital? Us at his funeral? Him not coming to my end of sophomore year photo display, not coming to Vantage Point, not taking me to the bus terminal when I went to New York, not coming to pick me up. Memories of everything he missed.

But those things still happened. I still took photos. Mom and I are still here, incomplete but still a family. I flip through the old photos, sorting through my thoughts.

I need to make that yearbook. Not for Dad, but for Mom and for me. For us to move on.

I start up his huge Mac, the one he used for all his editing work. He always kept a running folder marked Yearbook, where he'd load the good photos during the year, his and mine. I find it and click. He'd started it—creating separate folders inside the main one for each month. I click on January and scroll through the photos. Then I close it and click through the following months. When I get to May, it's empty. The month he was hospitalized. June's empty too. The month he died. And then I see one folder that doesn't belong. It's not a month at all. Instead, it says DW. My fingers are trembling as I click on it. There's got to be at least 200 photos in it. I open the first one. It's me as a baby, maybe a few weeks old; the same photo hangs from the wall on the second-floor landing. I click on the next. Me again, about a year old, standing in the back-yard. I click and click and click. All pictures of me, growing up. Was Dad going to make an album for David? Because he was dying? Because he wanted him to have something of me?

My instinct is to shut down the computer, to ignore this information. But even once I'm out of the darkroom, thoughts of these photos, these projects my dad had started, fill my mind. No amount of homework or TV distractions can shut out what I've seen. There's something about it—this was impor-tant to my dad, sure, but there's something else too. I lie in bed trying to work through it, too restless to sleep. Maybe it's that I'm the only one who knows these unfinished projects exist.

Finding out that David's my father, that my mother kept it a secret, that my dad did too, Mom wanting me to talk to David, seeing David with Savida: everything has been happening *to* me, totally out of my control. But these projects that Dad started? It's up to me what happens. I can decide to finish the yearbook that he started, to continue the tradition. I can create an album for David, a gift from my father—and a gesture that acknowledges who he is to me. I have the choice, finally. I feel a lightness and a sense of calm, but instead of finally drifting off to sleep, I'm energized. The house is dark—Mom is asleep—and I tiptoe downstairs and back into the darkroom. I start up the computer again and open the first folder.

CHAPTER 16: ELEVEN DAYS UNTIL I'M OVER HIM

Dace sideswipes me on my way out of last period. "You're coming home with me. No excuses."

I shake my head and try to break free from her death grip. "I have to go home. I—"

"You've been spending every single minute in that darkroom. Gemma told me you skipped photo club this week and I heard Jeffrey gloating you're giving him all your *Hall Pass* bylines. Have you forgotten you need that stuff for your college apps? And you're starting to look like a snowball. It's not healthy," she says as we walk outside. "Your skin's all pasty white and uneven. What you need is a change of scenery and a vitamin C peel. Also, without your nagging, I haven't been doing my homework. The novelty of my school supplies has worn off. Not even scrolling through photos of cars helps. I need moral support. You don't need to do anything, you just need to be there. To keep me in check."

The wind is whipping through my coat, and the thought of walking home makes me feel cold and lonely. I've spent the past two weeks locked away in the darkroom, but both the Greene Family Yearbook and the album for David are basically done. And so I give in, and we hole up in her room, with hot chocolate, marshmallows and chocolate chip cookies. I'm just setting up on the bed with my Geography textbook when Dace says tentatively, "Hey, can we talk about something?" She moves from her desk to the bed.

"Of course." I push my homework aside and arrange myself so I'm sitting cross-legged in front of her. "What's up?"

"It's . . . about Juan. I broke up with him."

"When? Why? I thought you really liked him."

"Yeah well, I did, and I thought everything was totally cool after the party, but then he started acting all weird about our age difference. I was so caught up in me breaking my own rules and going for a younger guy, I never considered he might have his own rules."

"Wow, he said that?"

"No, which is kind of the point. If he had, I might have respected him more, but he said it didn't matter to him, but that his friends have been giving him a hard time about dating me because I'm older. Like, what the Fudgsicle? Man up, little boy. So I told him it was over. I'm not going to date someone who lets his friends dictate his life."

"Wow. So that's it?" I take a sip of hot chocolate. "I'm impressed. You're so much stronger than me when it comes to relationships."

"Shut the front door. You are stronger than you

ever give yourself credit for. And anyways, that's kind of my point. Like, I think I made a mistake. I'm miserable. I really like him and instead of fighting for him I took the chicken way out."

"Then you have to follow your heart. Don't give him the easy way out by breaking up with him. Tell him you want to be his girlfriend and that he's going to have to deal with his friends if he wants to be your boyfriend."

"You're right," Dace says with gusto. "Good pep talk. OK, let's get to work. Actually, wait, one more thing." She leans over and grabs her phone off the desk. "Want to see some of the shots from the Nordstrom shoot?"

"Of course! I'm sorry—I didn't even ask you how it went." I hunch over her phone.

Dace scrolls through a few shots. "Everyone was really cool to work with, and the feedback's been good, so hopefully it becomes a semi-regular thing. Looks cool though, right?"

"Really cool. Ooh, I love this skirt on you," I say, pointing at a knee-length fuchsia eyelet number.

"Me too. Totally wanted to steal it from the shoot." We reach the last pic, and she pushes herself off the bed and goes over to the desk, then flips open her laptop.

I turn back to my homework. We work away silently. After a while, I stand to stretch and realize we've been at it for nearly two hours; it's been nice to have company after being alone for the past few weeks.

My phone dings and I swipe at the screen to see

the Instagram notification. Ramona tagged me in a photo. I heart it, then she writes back instantly, *Miss you roomie. Miss you too*, I reply. Out of habit, I go to Dylan's page, then flip to Muse's. There's a photo of two plates on red plastic placements and the caption: *Dumpee diner date with my non-boyfriend.* She's tagged *DylMc*.

I show Dace. "So now they're bonding over being dumped. Wow, I'm so glad I gave him something else to have in common with Muse," I say sarcastically.

Dace squints at the screen, then grabs the phone from me. "It doesn't mean anything. She says *right there* he's not her boyfriend." She hands my phone back.

"That's exactly what you say when you're flirting and trying to make a point, like, *Hey why* aren't *we together?*" I shake my head. "It feels hopeless. I'm gonna go," I say, tossing my phone in my bag and slinging it over my shoulder. "Thanks for trying to cheer me up. And I'm sorry I've been a bad friend lately." She follows me down the stairs and watches as I pull on my coat and boots.

She buttons my coat, then holds my face in her hands. "You're my best friend. That's what I'm here for. You're going to get through this. And hey," she says as I turn to go, "don't shut your mom out either, OK? I bet she wants to be there for you. It's easier to let her than to fight it."

I nod. Mom's been trying to get me out of my funk for weeks too, leaving my favorite foods—mac 'n' cheese with crushed chips on top, hot chocolate with a scoop of peanut butter, Cheetos—outside the darkroom or my bedroom door, switching shifts so she can be home when I get home from school, filling the empty air with idle chatter, and I've given her nothing but that one sobfest in return. I couldn't bear to get into the whole thing with her that night and haven't wanted to since.

The walk home is snowy, but the air is warmer than it's been in weeks. The moon is nearly full and visible in the dark, late afternoon sky. I grab the mail on my way inside, tossing it on the table inside the front door before bending to pull off my boots. A white envelope escapes the rest, and I pick it up, then notice the return address. *D. Westerly.* I turn it over. Mom's name is handwritten on the front.

I should just put the envelope back on the stack and pretend I never saw it, but I can't. I have to know what he's sending her. Is this some old-school romance? "Mom?" I call, my voice wavering. But the house is empty. I look at the envelope again, and then run up the stairs to the bathroom, where the lighting's best. I flip on the overhead and mirror lights, then hold the envelope up in the air. For a split second I thought the idea would be silly, that I'd have to resort to steaming the envelope open, like they do on TV shows. Or putting whatever's inside into another identical envelope and forging his handwriting. But the slip of paper inside the envelope is as clear as if there wasn't even an envelope.

It's a check. Made out to Holly Greene, in trust for Philadelphia Greene. For a lot of money.

Despite my one get-out-of-the-darkroom day, I head straight back home to the basement the next day after school. I still haven't talked to Mom about the check, but I will. First, I need to finish the album. A few hours later, I add it to the cart on the photobook site where I'd already uploaded the Greene Family Yearbook. I enter our address and complete the order, then push Dad's chair back and get up.

The door closes solidly, and I tuck the key in my pocket.

Upstairs, I find my phone under a pile of papers on my desk. David answers on the third ring. My heart's pounding so loud I can barely hear myself speak.

"Hi. David? It's Pippa." I sit down on the edge of my bed.

"Pippa." He sounds genuinely happy to hear from

me, and my heart starts to slow its rapid rate. "I'm glad you called. I'm in the middle of a nightmare shoot, and I could use an excuse to get away from these maniacs. What's up?"

I've been thinking about telling him for weeks, and now I finally am. I take a deep breath and plunge on before I lose my nerve. "I . . . know. Um, I . . . know you're my biological father."

Silence. I can hear him shuffling around, and he tells me he's going into the hallway for privacy. The sound of the metal door to his studio closes and he exhales. "OK that's better." Pause. "About knowing. I'm glad. I really am. God, it was so hard not to say anything when you were here in New York, asking a million questions about your mother, about Evan. About your father." Pause. "This is hard on the phone. But I . . . want you to know I'm sorry I did what I did. I'm sorry I abandoned your mother. God, I was an asshole. And I'm sorry I abandoned you."

"It's OK," I say, because I don't know what else to say.

He sort of half-laughs. "No, it's not OK, but I appreciate you saying that. And I'm so grateful to Evan, because he was the father I never could've been. So thank god for him, but I'm not off the hook. I failed. Big time. I'd like to say I'll make it up to you, but I can't make up 16 years." David pauses, and I hear him talking to someone else. I slide off the edge of my bed until I'm on the floor, my back against the bed frame. His words settling. A minute later, he says my name. A question.

"Hi. I'm still here." I pick at a tuft of carpet.

"Your mom suggested maybe I could see you again sometime, play a role in your life somehow. Not to replace your father. Just be a guy who cares. Who thinks you're a really cool girl. And a goddamn great photographer." He pauses. "A daughter your parents must be proud of." There's a hint of sadness in his voice, the way he says "parents," not referring to himself.

"OK," I say. Which is pretty much the shortest answer I could possibly give, but it's all I can muster at the moment. Noncommittal, but not closing the door either. He doesn't mention the check, and neither do I.

"I should go," I say, but then I pause, not going, and so David asks how school is, and I say OK, and then I tell him about the reunion project I'm working on but not really working on, and then in that pause, because I can't bring myself to tell him I've been locked in the darkroom for weeks, he asks how my boyfriend is.

And I start to cry, which feels like all I've been doing lately.

I think about telling him what happened, or didn't happen, but I can't talk at all. Finally, I catch my breath.

"I bet that feels better, huh?" he says, finally. And I laugh.

"What does your mother think?" David asks.

And suddenly I don't know why I haven't talked to her about it.

● ● ●

Mom's in her bedroom, changing the sheets on her bed. A laundry hamper sits at the foot. All the furniture's still slightly pushed toward the center of the room, away from the walls. They're still half peach, half white, the paint long put away, as though she's resigned herself to this new décor. Which means what—that I win? I don't want to win anymore, because it just feels like losing her.

"Hey," I say, suddenly feeling nervous as I edge open the door.

"Hi." She holds a pillow with her chin, wriggling the fresh pillowcase over it.

"I talked to David."

She gives the pillow a couple of good shakes and then tosses it at the headboard. "Want to sit?" She nods at the bed.

"Not really. I was thinking maybe, I could help you fix this?" I gesture to the wall closest to me.

"You don't have to do that."

"I want to help. I feel like it's my fault you stopped painting." I roll my eyes. "OK, I *know* it's my fault."

"Right now? I don't have any other paint. Just the peach."

"Then we'll paint it peach. Like James."

She grabs the comforter off the floor and I help her pull it over the sheets. "I haven't thought about that book in forever. Your dad and I used to read it to you at bedtime; he'd do all the voices."

"So can we?"

She opens the closet door and pulls out all the painting stuff. "Good cleanup job, right?" she says, then hands me one of Dad's big shirts. "So you don't wreck your clothes."

"Thanks," I say, pulling the dress shirt over top of my sweater dress and rolling up the sleeves. I pull my hair into a ponytail, securing it with the elastic on my wrist. "Want one?" I say offering her another elastic. She takes the elastic and puts her hair up too.

"We should listen to music," I say. "Everything should be set to a soundtrack."

"You're going to have to be in charge of that."

Dad always handled music in the house—I don't think Mom even has an iTunes account. But when he died, we got rid of his cellphone. And with it, his music.

That's the thing about death you don't really consider. What do you do with someone's cellphone? Their Instagram account? Their email address? Seems other people don't really know either—Mom spent hours on the phone with the cellphone company, arguing about discontinuing his plan. You'd think they'd waive the fee for breaking the contract when someone dies. We never took down his website. I'm sure his inbox is full of wedding requests from soon-to-be married couples, wondering why that great photographer they heard about hasn't replied.

My phone's in my room and I return with it and my iPod dock, which I set up on Mom's dresser and press shuffle. Mom starts covering up all the furniture again, using the drop sheets. The paintbrush feels heavy in my hand, then heavier after I dip it into the paint.

"I don't hate the peach," I say awhile later, once I've trimmed the length of one wall.

Eventually, I tell Mom about Dylan. The details. About Muse. And then I tell her about Savida. The girl in our group, a senior from New York, who I found on the roof of David's building, during his party, kissing David, the guy who's supposed to be a father figure to me. And how that was a big part of my reluctance to call him. To let him back into my life, when it was so much easier to just have him out of sight, out of mind now that I wasn't in New York.

Mom listens as I tell her everything. There are breaks where we're not talking, just painting opposite walls. And then I'll think of something else to say, another anecdote to share. Through it all, she listens, and then she surprises me. She doesn't offer her advice or an opinion or try to discount anything I'm saying, or even try to agree with me. Instead, she lets out a deep breath and then says, "You've had to deal with a lot this year."

"I saw the check," I add.

"From David," Mom clarifies.

"Yes."

"I probably should've told you. But I . . . well, I didn't want to sway your feelings about him, or make you feel obligated to him in any way. You were right to feel how you felt about him, and I was already asking a lot of you. But after meeting you, well, I think it really hit home with him, that you were his daughter. That even though he hadn't been a father to you, he *was* your father. *Is* your father. He wanted to send some money. For your future."

"For Tisch."

"For whatever you choose to do. He actually just wanted to send me money to help out with"—she waves her hand around—"life, but I told him no. He insisted and then we agreed only if it was in trust for you. So that it had to be spent on tuition or your first apartment or something you need."

"Why didn't he tell—" I don't finish my thought.

"He didn't want you to know it was coming from him."

We paint in silence some more. At some point my playlist ends, and the only sound is the *whishing* of our roller brushes.

"Can I ask you something?" I say. "How long did it take for you to get over breaking up with David?"

"Oh honey," Mom says. "I'm so sorry about you and Dylan."

"I broke up with him, but it's like every single day I want to be with him. I keep checking my phone to see if he's texted, and I can't stop looking at his Instagram page, for what? A clue that he misses me? It's pure torture. Especially because I think he might have already moved on."

Mom puts down her paintbrush and comes over and hugs me. She holds me like that for longer than she needs to without saying anything, and I'm glad. Then she pulls away and looks at me. "You still love him, sweetheart. You broke up with the guy he was being, but you still love the Dylan he used to be. You're mourning the loss of *that* guy. Am I right?"

I nod. And then I get it. That's what it was like for her and David.

"I don't want to say anything that makes you think I wasn't totally, completely in love with your father. Because that wouldn't be true. What your father and I had, we grew into. A slow, great love. But it doesn't mean there wasn't this period—and remember, I had just had you, my hormones were raging—where I missed David and our relationship. That love made you."

I sigh. "So how did you finally get over him?"

"Time," she says simply. "I had you, and you took up a lot of my focus, but as you started to grow, your father, you and I became this family. And I forgot David was ever really a part of it. Of me." She pauses. "The other thing was, I had no way of checking up on David. Remember this was way back before email, texting, tweeting, Instagram. He was out of sight, and eventually out of mind. And that really did help me to forget about him." She puts an arm around me. "What if you tried to go old school? Take a break. Log out of your Instagram so you're not tempted to look at his page. Or leave your phone at home some days? Is that even possible?" Her eyes bug out, and she laughs.

I laugh. "I don't know. Maybe?"

She offers a small smile. "I don't want to see you lose yourself in your heartbreak, Pip. Just remember that you have always been more than just someone's girlfriend."

"Thanks, Mom. For everything. I know I haven't exactly been the easiest person to live with lately."

Mom grins, then claps her hands. "I'm hungry. Are you hungry?"

"Yeah," I say.

"How about Pete's? We could get takeout, bring it back here and watch a movie."

It's been ages since we've had Pete's. After Dad died we had to cut back on a lot, and that meant terrible frozen pizza instead of takeout from Pete's. But I think it wasn't only about pinching pennies: Mom also couldn't bring herself to go on doing the things the three of us used to do. But it's kind of like how I feel with the yearbook—I don't think either one of us wants to lose all our traditions, along with Dad.

I grab the takeout menu from the corkboard beside the fridge. It's where we keep all our important emergency numbers. Mom hasn't updated it in, like, seven years—it still has Anita's number, the babysitter who used to watch me until I turned 10 and Mom and Dad determined I could stay home by myself.

"You want to drive?" Mom asks. I look at her in surprise. She never lets me drive.

●　●　●

Pete's always smells like a mix of spiciness and sweetness, just like the Hawaiian pizza we ordered. The décor hasn't been updated since it opened decades ago—the top half of the walls are deep red, the bottom half wainscoted in dark wood. Somehow the black linoleum floors are still shiny after all these years.

I walk up to the counter and recognize the back of the guy in front of me. I tap his shoulder.

"Hey," Ben says, grinning when he sees it's me. "You're alive!"

I roll my eyes.

"I was about to start flyering the town with your face. Who are you here with?" He looks around. The guy at the counter hands him a wad of brown paper napkins.

"My mom. She's in the car. I'm just picking up our pizza. Who are you here with?"

"Yeah, my mom too. It's her birthday, so the boys and I are taking her out for pizza. My stepdad's away on business."

The guy at the counter looks at me expectantly, and I give him my last name. He tells me the pizza'll still be another five minutes.

"The boys?" I say, and he points to a table with a woman, who I guess is his mom, and two boys, about five or six.

"My little brothers. You want to meet them?"

I shrug. "Sure," I say, feeling nervous for some reason. I follow him over to the table. He puts the wad of paper napkins down on the wet table and his mom wipes up the water. "Aidan's six, Alex is almost five. This is Pippa. Say hi," he commands gruffly, which makes me laugh. "Hi Pippa," they sing-song in unison. "And my mom. Mom, this is Pippa. Her mom is the one who works at the vet clinic."

"Oh! Is she here? I'd love to meet her and thank her personally."

"She's in the car." I thumb toward the door. "I can tell her to come in."

"If she wouldn't mind! We just ordered—do you want to eat with us?"

"I can ask, I guess," I say.

For a split second I consider standing in the heated foyer, then telling Ben's mom that my mom says we can't stay. But truthfully, it would be kind of *nice* to sit inside and eat with Ben's family. I think both Mom and I could use a break from the house.

"Everything OK?" Mom says when I approach the car.

"Mrs. Baxter wants to say hi." I realize as I say it that her last name might not be Baxter anymore, if she's remarried. "Ben's mom? The one with Catniss the cat?"

"Oh, Veronica! I'd love to meet her. Is she inside?" I nod, and Mom follows me back inside. Soon Ben's mom is reiterating the offer to eat with them. Mom glances at me, I smile and she says, "That sounds lovely."

Veronica tells Ben to find two more chairs in the busy restaurant, and then she flags down a waiter and we order drinks.

"Jukebox?" Ben suggests after returning with the chairs, and I follow him over, winding our way through the tables. Even though it's a Tuesday, Pete's is packed. It always is, with people of all ages, but especially in winter when the patio is closed.

"How's ski club?"

"Awesome. I haven't seen this much new powder, consistently, in years."

"I hadn't even really noticed," I say, realizing what a bubble I've been living in.

"Yeah, you've been pretty MIA. Even from photo club. You OK?"

I nod. "I think this is the beginning of the end

of my funk. At least, I can get back to the alumni project. Sorry I abandoned you and Gemma on it."

He shrugs. "Break-ups suck. Have you heard from Dylan at all?"

I shake my head. "I think he's dating this girl Muse."

"Bangs? Black hair?" Ben asks.

I nod.

"I saw him with that girl the other day. At the movies."

I bite my lip to hold back the tears. It doesn't work.

Ben pulls a napkin from a dispenser on the nearest table and passes it to me. I dab my eyes with it and take a deep breath.

"I heard this theory," I tell him. "That it takes a quarter of the time you were with someone to get over them."

"Really," Ben says evenly.

"Yeah, well," I say. "It doesn't appear to apply to Dylan McCutter."

I wonder what Dylan's doing right now. Without realizing it, I feel almost as though, when I was inside working on the photo albums, my life was on hold—or life, in general, was on hold. But now that I'm out in the world, seeing people laughing and eating pizza on a Tuesday, it feels like I can't pretend. Dylan hasn't been waiting outside my door for me. He's living his life. He's moved on.

"It's weird," I say. "I broke up with him. Isn't the person who does the breaking up—the breaker-upper—supposed to be OK? Like, I wanted to break up with him otherwise I wouldn't have broken up with him, so why am I so sad?"

"There's this theory about manufactured foods," Ben says, and I raise my eyebrows. He holds up a hand. "Hear me out. We like foods that have an identifiable strong flavor, but we tire of them quickly. Salt 'n' vinegar chips, chocolate, root beer. It's exciting at first, and then it fizzles out. But Coke . . . Coke is different. Apparently it's perfectly engineered so that you don't tire of it."

"The point, Baxter. The point."

"Maybe our dating instincts are like our taste-buds. Why so many people hook up for a night but never again. Or go out for a month and then break up. It's why it takes so long to find someone to be with forever, I guess."

"So you think Dylan's not Coke."

"I don't mean to make him sound like a simple can of soda."

"Dace also has a theory about soda. And that Coke boys are the best. The whole package. But they're kept that way because Pepsis are always close behind, vying to be the favorite."

"Where does that leave Orange Crush?" Ben asks.

"Somewhere between cream soda and root beer, I guess."

"Better than ginger ale."

I run my fingers over the jukebox keys. "I was so sure that we were *meant* to be together." The jukebox has this ornamental feature around the display, illuminated fluid-filled tubes through which bubbles rise. I watch one speed toward the top, where it breaks to join the surface air. "Anyway, can we talk about something else?"

"Taylor Swift's new hairstyle. Love or hate?"

I laugh. "Love, obvs. So the project. How's it coming along?"

He shrugs. "I've gotten a lot of quotes from alumni and students about their memories—that Facebook page was brilliant, if I can take all the credit, but the taking of pictures . . . well, I was hoping you'd resurface in time to get at it?"

Oh crap, I think.

"Oh crap," I say. "Gemma didn't shoot anything?"

"Gemma's kind of not on the project anymore."

"What happened?"

"Well—we broke up."

"You broke up?" I say. "I really was living under a rock. Sorry."

"We weren't each other's Cokes." He punches a quarter into the jukebox and picks a song from the '80s. "One of my mom's favorites," he explains. "I actually brought my camera tonight. I remembered you saying this place has been a hangout for Spalding students for years."

"Decades."

"Great, I'll just grab my camera."

I watch him, his easy strides, and a funny feeling emerges inside me. I realize I'm really happy to see him. Or maybe I'm just super hungry?

"So, what's inherently Pete's?" Ben asks once he's jukebox-adjacent once more.

"Well, I mean, the pizza, but that's pretty obvious. What about this jukebox?"

"Duh," Ben says. "Could it have been any more obvious?"

"Let's do a close-up on one of the buttons," I say, and Ben hands over his camera.

"You shoot it."

I take the camera and lean close, focusing on the K. I snap a few frames, then hold the camera out so we can both see. "Hmm. I don't love it."

"What about focusing in on the P. For Pete's?"

"Better idea," I say, then refocus. I snap a few more, changing the angle of view to get the flipbook of song titles into the shot.

"Wow, that's great," Ben says when I show him.

"Hey, so ski club—is there room for one more? Asking for a friend."

"Tell your friend yes. She'll love it."

● ● ●

"You still thinking about Tisch for college?" We're in Ben's car. After convincing his mom and my mom to go out to celebrate Veronica's birthday, they took a cab and left Mom's car at Pete's, and Ben's driving me home. The boys are in the backseat.

"Definitely," I say, my finger on the seat-warmer button. "I miss it. It's crazy how two weeks changes everything."

"Yeah," he says, and I feel guilty.

"I probably owe you an apology for that. You would've gone away snowboarding all winter and instead you're stuck at Spalding. Like, who am I to tell you what to do?"

His expression is unreadable in the short glance he throws my way before he turns his attention back to the road.

"Actually, I was going to thank you for that," Ben says. "It felt—nice. To have someone making me feel wanted, or like I belong somewhere, you know? Especially with my dad not caring. And my mom— well, she's great, but between the problems we've had with my 'acting out' and the boys and her work . . . and her obsession with decorating our home . . ."

I laugh. And Ben laughs. "You think I'm kidding but she has a real obsession. You'll see."

"How will I see?"

"Oh yeah, right. That was in my head."

"What was?"

"When I asked if you wanted to come over and check out my record player. Which, wow, that sounds like a line. But it's not. The NADINATOR will change your life. Come on. Unless you really want to get home."

"Yeah, I'm dying to get home after being out of the house doing something other than school for the first time in, like, 17 days."

He turns left at the light and then right on the first side street, then pulls into the driveway of a large, two-story brick home. Ben's house is in Spalding Heights. It's not anything like Luis and Juan Juarez's or some of the other sprawling homes in the area, but it's still really nice. It's dark brick, and all the windows have white edging around them. The front door is massive with one of those brass lion knockers.

"Upstairs, and into your PJs," Ben instructs the boys when we get inside. They kick off their boots and drop their hats, mitts and coats inside the front door and race up the stairs.

"Wow," I say once we're inside. The hall foyer is open up to the second floor, with a massive crystal chandelier that hangs down from the second-story ceiling. The walls of the hallway are lined in mirrors, making it feel like we're in the palace of Versailles. Or at least, how I imagine it from seeing pictures in my history textbook. "This is a beautiful house."

"That's one way to describe it," Ben says, then gestures to the floor. "White carpets! Who puts in white carpets?" He nods at the mat by the door. "Which is why we must take our shoes off here."

"Sure." Instead of kicking off my boots the way I do at home, I bend over and gingerly remove them, then stand them up on the mat.

He leads me up the stairs to his room and pushes open the door. The room is square with a large window that overlooks the backyard. His bed is trunk-style, with worn-looking dark wood drawers that pull out under the mattress and what looks like faux-vintage baseball striped bedding. There's a large framed bulletin board with ticket stubs on one wall and on the other wall is a huge map of the world, one of those novelty maps that you can scratch off the places you've been.

"You've traveled a lot."

He nods. "Yeah, before Dad left, we used to travel with him."

Over his bed is a red star lit by tiny clear bulbs.

The shelves are cage-like, and at the end of his bed there's a trunk filled with old LPs.

"This could be in a magazine," I say, looking around.

He nods. "Or a catalog, right?" He walks over to his desk, which is dark wood and has one of those rolling desk chairs. He grabs a Restoration Hardware catalog—and opens it to a spread of his room.

The only difference is the cast-iron letter on the bookshelf—a B instead of an E.

"Wow," I laugh.

"She's already planning what she's going to do with it when I move out."

"What are you going to do after high school?"

"That's the million-dollar question," he says. "But the answer, you're going to have to wait for. I've got to go read the boys bedtime stories. You want to come?"

"Sure," I say nervously, following him down the hall. His brothers have an equally exquisitely deco-rated room.

"Page 34," Ben explains. He pulls over two beanbag chairs, giving me a navy one that says *Aidan* in red letters and plopping himself down in a red one that says *Alex* in navy letters.

"OK, five pages of your choice, then five pages of mine," he says, and the boys scream, "Captain Underpants!" in unison.

"Surprising," Ben says sarcastically as Aidan drops the book over the top bunk. Ben catches it and opens it to the folded page. He reads, holding up the book to show both kids the pictures every few seconds. A few minutes later he folds the corner of the page and puts the book aside, then grabs another from the dresser behind him, holding it up for me to see. "Hardy Boys. My pick. Who wants to fill Pippa in on where we left off?" Aidan explains that the boys have just run after a bad guy who went to the train station.

Ben reads and I close my eyes, listening to the story.

When he finishes he stands, then holds his hand out to me to pull me out of the beanbag. He climbs up the bunk to kiss Aidan and then lowers himself to Alex's bunk. He joins me in the hall and we walk back to his room.

"OK, what would you like to listen to?" Ben goes over to the shelf beside his bed and lifts the lid on his record player.

"Something I don't know." I sit down on his plush carpet, my back against the wall.

Ben rifles through his albums and I look around the room, scanning the shelves. The entire Hardy Boys collection, the old-fashioned hardcover books, line the top shelf of his room, above his desk. On his dresser are a bunch of different bottles—aftershave and cologne and hair gel and deodorant.

He slips an LP out of its sleeve and onto the turntable. "This band's pretty obscure, but they've got this one song. My dad used to listen to this album when I was little. This line—" He turns the volume up. "It's about a relationship but it makes me think of my dad now."

"Like closure?" I ask, but he shakes his head.

"That's the thing, I guess I was looking for closure, but maybe not everything in life gets it, you know? Some stuff just *is*. I don't know. Maybe that's my way of resigning myself to what happened with him."

"I'm sorry about the way things turned out," I say, stretching my legs out in front of me. Ben risked a lot to go to New York to find his dad, because to him, it was worth it. Only the reason his mother had banned him from making contact turned out to be for his own good—his dad just didn't want Ben in his life. Simple and sad as that.

"Me too," Ben says, turning the LP jacket over in his hands. "But in a way it's better just to know. Does that make sense?"

"Yeah," I say, thinking about Dylan. How being without him sucks, but maybe it's better to know how he feels, to know where I stand. To have made the choice to be apart, even if that clears the way for Muse and Dylan to get together. I instinctively reach for my phone. Maybe Mom was right. Maybe I do need an Instagram break. "Limbo. It sucks."

"Exactly. That's how I felt all these years too. And yeah, it sucks to not be wanted by my dad, but at the same time, it's somehow brought me closer to my mom. It made me realize that being a parent, being a good parent, it's a choice."

He gets up and grabs two pillows off his bed, then hands me one and puts the other against the wall, and then he stretches out so he's lying down on his back, looking up at the ceiling, his head on the pillow. I pull my knees to my chin, hugging the pillow between my legs and chest.

"I told David I know."

Ben lets out a whistle and looks over at me. "How'd that go?"

"Fine, as boring as that sounds. Now we all know. I guess that's why my mom wanted me to do it. It actually does feel like a relief." I stretch out and tuck the pillow under my head, staring up at the ceiling too, Ben an arm's length away.

"I guess both our moms had methods to their madness. And I'm happy to still be at Spalding. I've got ski club, and my classes aren't bad this term. And—" He stops. Whatever he was about to say, he decides against it.

For a while, we lie on the carpet, listening to the music. The record ends and we still lie there— the sound of the turntable, Ben's breathing and mine. It's the calmest I've felt in weeks. At some point, Veronica comes home and upstairs; she pokes her head around Ben's open bedroom door. "Rise and shine, you crazy kids. It's late and a school night." Ben's just as dopey as I am, and I wonder if he fell asleep.

Ben drives me home and we're quiet in the car. He pulls into my driveway and puts the car in park. And then there's the awkward how-will-we-say-goodnight moment. But Ben breaks it. "I'll text you about the alumni photos."

"Cool. Thanks for the ride."

I get out and walk up to the front door. Ben waits

in the driveway until I'm inside, and there's only a moment that I wish it had been Dylan I had spent my night with.

CHAPTER 18: ONE WEEK UNTIL I'M OVER HIM

Ski club members get out of class 20 minutes early on Friday, and by the time I get to the coach bus out front, Dace is already on board and has saved me a seat beside her, behind Gemma and Emma. "Always sitting behind twins, huh?" Ben says as he passes me.

"What's he talking about?" Dace asks, but I just roll my eyes and laugh.

Everyone's talking and laughing, and for the first time in a long time, I feel like I'm really part of something, in a way I haven't felt since Tisch Camp.

"I'm so glad you're here," Dace says, squeezing my arm. "Even if it had to come at the loss of The McCuter."

"Let's talk about something else, kay?"

"Done. The dance. We haven't even discussed wardrobe!"

"Yeah," I say, disheartened. Of course I'm still going to go—how can I not, given I'm doing the mural—but it feels hard to get excited about going when I'd pictured Dylan and me going to our first high school dance together.

"We should probably shop for dresses together," Dace is saying. "To make sure we're not matchy-matchy, but we're also not clashy-clashy." She purses her lips and bats her eyelashes at me.

"I was thinking you'd probably want to go with Juan."

"Juan who?"

"Really?" Typically when Dace breaks up with a guy, he tries for months to win back her affections.

Dace shrugs it off. "He's still being an idiot. I have no time for that. Anyway, you're my best friend. Besties before the resties. So: dresses. I made a Pinterest board, obvs," she says, pulling out her phone. "Want to see?"

"Yes," I say, laughing and leaning back in my seat.

The hour to the hill passes by in a flash, and then we're out in the winter wonderland. Everyone in ski club gets a lesson included in their lift ticket. Dace is in an intermediate class, but she shows me to my group first before going to hers. She wishes me good luck, tells me not to break anything and reminds me everyone meets inside the lodge at 6 to eat before skiing together for the remainder of the evening until the bus leaves to go home at 10:30.

Skiing isn't exactly like riding a bike but I do remember a bit from winter break, and no one laughs at me, and I don't fall that many times. And when the lesson is over, I still want to keep skiing, so I feel like it's a success.

I'm looking around for a clock, when someone comes up beside me. He releases his foot from his snowboard, puts his goggles on top of his white helmet and grins. "Wanna do one more run before we go in? We have about 20 minutes," Ben says. "Come on, I'll take you on a real hill."

"I'm not ready for a real hill," I say.

"Of course you are. Trust me, it's even easier than the bunny hill."

He starts off toward the next chairlift, and I dig my poles in to keep up.

I slide into line for the chairlift with him and try not to freak out.

Ben sort of takes up a lot of space and we end up alone on the chairlift, which is fine with me, because the worst part of skiing is sitting four to a lift and trying to not knock everyone down when you get off at the top.

Ben lowers the bar on the chair and leaves his arm on the back of the seat, behind me. As we ride up the lift, Ben asks me if I have any plans for spring break, which I don't, and then says he's going to Park City to snowboard with his brothers and stepdad. "Although I have a funny feeling we'll be spending a lot of time in the hotel arcade. You know, it's fine. It'll be fun with them. Besides, they've been brushing up on their jokes for the trip. They're practicing on each other, to surprise Ted. I can hardly wait."

"Do they tell funny jokes?"

"You be the judge. Knock knock."

I laugh. "Who's there?"

"Knock knock."

"Who's there?" I say again.

"Knock. *Knock.*" Ben waves his hands in the air, a *c'mon* moment.

"Who's there?" I laugh.

"I keep telling you, my name is Knock Knock! So why don't you answer the door?"

I laugh.

"Stop it, it's not even funny."

"It's a little funny."

"I give them a rating out of 10 every time they tell me a joke."

"What did this one get?"

"Two."

"Wow, that's harsh."

"All knock-knock jokes automatically lose five points for being knock-knock jokes."

The top of the chairlift—where we have to get off—is five poles away. "Ready?" he asks, bringing his arm down to the bar in front of us.

"Define ready. I'm totally nervous."

"Don't worry. It's nerves that make you fall. Just take a deep breath, go straight. Lean forward. And give me one of your poles." Then he lifts the bar. "Let's do it." He stands and pulls on my pole, steadying me and I follow his instructions. And stay standing.

"I did it!" I cheer, and then realize that getting off the chairlift is just something people do and even though I totally rocked it, I could be a bit cooler about it.

Ben laughs, hobbles over to an area out of the way, sits down in the snow and straps his boot back in, then gets up. "Ready? I'm going to make nice wide turns across the hill. Just follow my tracks the best you can. Nice and slow."

I'm skeptical as he takes off. For one, he's on a snowboard. I've seen snowboarders go down the mountain—*how* they go down the mountain, snow flying, basically going straight down. And he's a billion times better than me, I'm sure, but he does exactly what he says and starts off really slow, making these wide turns like I've never seen any snowboarder—ever—perform. I focus on the track he's making in the snow—at this point in the day there's a million tracks all over the hill, but I can see where he's made a fresh one. I veer off at one point, unable to make the turn because of a looming patch of ice, but I do eventually turn and Ben calls out words of encouragement and tells me to catch the track again.

Ten minutes later, I let myself go straight at the base to where he's standing. He whoops. "That was impressive!"

I smile, proud of myself. "I was wrong: you should've run off to be a ski instructor—you're awesome at this positive reinforcement thing."

He smiles back at me. "Let's go in for dinner. I'm starving." He bends over and in one quick snap, he unhinges his feet from his board and swings the board over his shoulder. "Here," he says, grabbing one of my poles and quickly stabbing behind me. A second later, my boots are free too. "You take your skis and I'll take your poles," he says, and I follow him over to the chalet. We stash our stuff at one of the metal racks and he clips a lock onto the bar at the top. "Just remind me we're locked up together," he says as we head inside.

Hot air blows in our faces as we pull open the doors. Dace is waving at us and we make our way over to the long wood table and benches where everyone from Spalding is converging. Goggles, helmets, neck warmers, gloves—they all get dumped into a massive pile on the table. Then we join the lineup for food. After that we're all planning the rest of the night and scarfing dinner.

We've got all our stuff on again when I remember Ben has his lock on my skis. "Hey Ben," I say, as he's wiping the inside of his goggles with a cloth.

"Right. You want to ski together a bit?"

"Actually," I say, waving a hand toward Dace, Gemma and Emma, who are all getting their stuff on a few rows over, "I made a plan with the girls. Kind of perfect for the quad chair, you know?"

"Awesome, have fun. See you at the bus—10:30."

"What's going on with Ben?" Emma asks once the four of us are on the chairlift. I try to look over at her, which is hard because we're all geared up and she's right beside me. "Seems like he's maybe into someone again." Emma looks from Gemma to me.

I can feel myself blushing, and I'm grateful for the cold air.

"He was never *not* into Pippa," Gemma says. "Why do you think we only dated for, like, five minutes? But whatever—I've moved on. No hard feelings, Pip." She pulls her phone out and tries to angle it so we're all in the frame. "Chelfie?"

I look confused. Dace translates: "Selfie on a chairlift, ski club newb."

"Want one for your account?" Gemma asks me.

"I gave up Instagram for Lent."

"Lent doesn't start for another two weeks or something. Besides, since when are you religious?"

"I'm not. But I believe in the power of not looking at your ex-boyfriend's Instagram. So cold turkey was the only way to do it."

CHAPTER 19: SIX DAYS UNTIL I'M OVER HIM

The albums arrive by FedEx on Saturday afternoon. I intend to take them up to my room before Mom can ask who was at the door, to save the yearbook and give it to Mom on Valentine's Day, but I can't wait to see how they look, so I rip open the package right at the front door. When I see how beautiful the hardcover book turned out, there's no way I can wait. The cover has a picture of Mom, Dad and me, taken on a picnic we had on Easter weekend. We'd rode our bikes along the waterfront trail, and then stopped at this grassy field filled with dandelions. Sure, they're weeds, but the effect was absolutely beautiful.

"Who was that?" Mom says, coming up the stairs from the basement. I turn and hand her the book. She takes it gingerly in both hands. "What's this?" She runs a hand over the smooth cover.

"An early Valentine's Day gift."

She walks over to the living room and sits on the couch. "Come sit with me," she says, and I follow her over to the couch. She turns the pages slowly, taking in every picture. Eventually we get to the end, the final picture. It's Mom and me, on Christmas Eve. It's not the traditional photo Dad would take of the three of us every year—Dad and Mom holding me up as I put the star on top of the tree. We've been doing that same photo every year since I was born. But this year was so hard—our first Christmas without Dad, and me being mad at her for the David secret; things were different, to say the least. Thankfully Mom invited Aunt Emmy to spend the holidays with us, which was good for so many reasons. It helped Mom a lot, I think, to get through things, but she also acted as a buffer between Mom and me while we were in the middle of our awkward silent-fight. Anyway, to get the star on top of the tree, Aunt Emmy and Mom tried to hoist me but I kept toppling over before I could reach the top. At one point the tree toppled over on us, which is actually how we ended up getting the star on top, and then the three of us pushed the tree back upright. Without Aunt Emmy there, Mom and I might've got in a fight or gotten frustrated and given up, but Aunt Emmy lightened the moment—making it fun.

I was so caught up in the whole ordeal I forgot to set up my camera, but later, Mom made hot cocoa— the old-school way, from scratch, on the stove— with large, fancy homemade marshmallows Emmy brought from New York, and Emmy took a picture of Mom and me, on the couch together. That night, for one night only, we let everything else go, and you can tell that in the photo. When I was making the album, it seemed like a fitting end to the year, and the photo book.

Mom closes the album and looks at me. "It's better than the green gorilla," she says. Her eyes are filled with tears.

"Green gorilla?"

"I never told you about the green gorilla your father gave me on our first Valentine's Day together?" She sort of laugh-cries. "Oh Pippa," she says, pulling me into her. She smells like dryer sheets, and I rest my head on her shoulder.

We get up; Mom goes into the kitchen but picks up the FedEx box from the floor along the way. "Oh, there's something still in here." She reaches into the box.

"Oh," I say, embarrassed. "It's for David. I think Dad was making it for him. Did you know?"

Surprise is written all over her face. "May I look at it?"

I tell her she can, but I don't want to. I'm not ready. I go up to my room and sit at my computer, then grab my phone and text Jeffrey to find out the theme for photo club this week.

He texts back a second later: crowds. I look through my computer to see if I have any photos that will work for the theme.

Mom knocks on the door.

"This is a really special thing that you did, sweetie," Mom says, coming in. She places the album on my desk and puts a hand on my back. "You're going to mail it to him?"

"Yeah, unless . . . do you think that's a bad idea?"

"I think it's a great idea. I do have another suggestion. And it's just that."

"OK," I say slowly.

"The reunion. What if you invited David to come? I'm sure he'd love to see where you go to school, and see the alumni mural. We could invite him here for dinner. He could see our house, get a sense of your life here. It might be good, for both of you. And then you could give the album to him in person."

"I'll think about it."

CHAPTER 20: FOUR DAYS UNTIL I'M OVER HIM

"Pippa, slow down."

"Mom. I'm going, like, 10 miles an hour." I pull into the school parking lot on Monday evening and shut off the ignition. "Anyway, it's almost 7 and you can't be late—you only get 15 minutes with each of my teachers."

She pulls the visor down, opens her lipstick and runs it along her upper lip, lower lip, then presses her lips together. "OK." We get out of the car and walk across the parking lot.

Once we're inside, it's like the first day of school in the front hallway—only instead of students, it's adults crisscrossing and merging like ants, staring intently at schedules and at the top of the doorways to check the room numbers.

"Hello Pippa," Ms. Su says, but there's a warning tone in her voice. She lowers her glasses on her nose. I know what she's implying. The school has a strict no-students-at-parent-teacher-interview-night policy.

"I got permission from Principal Forsythe to come tonight, to take pictures for the alumni dance mural."

"All right," she says and then flips through her box of A–G last names to find my interview schedule. She hands it to Mom. "Looks like Mr. Alderman is first."

"Portable 3," I say as we walk down the main hall to the back doors. "Do you want me to show you which one?"

"Sure," she says, putting the schedule in her purse.

Mr. Alderman is sitting at his desk, shuffling papers. He looks up as we enter and runs a hand through his mass of curly brown hair. "Oh good," he says, standing. "I was just trying to look busy. Long time no see, Pippa. And this must be . . ." His face flashes recognition as he comes around the side of his desk.

"Holly?" Surprise fills his voice.

"Hank." Mom mimics his surprise and her face lights up.

Hank? Holly?

Mom tucks her hair behind her ear. "When Pippa said she had Mr. Alderman . . . I thought, well, I knew you always wanted to be a teacher."

"Or a rockstar." He folds his gangly arms over his V-neck sweater.

"Or a rockstar." Mom chuckles. "That's right. Do you still play guitar?"

"Sold-out shows in the basement. My son and I have a band. The Aldermanboy band. I'm the man, he's the boy. He plays recorder. He's seven." He blushes, seeming to realize that he's rambling. "How about you? Still modeling?" He puts his hands in the pockets of his gray cords.

"Oh no, I gave that up ages ago." She looks over at me, as though remembering I'm standing right beside her. I give a little wave. "Pippa, did you know Hank—Mr. Alderman—and I went to Spalding together?"

"No. I did not know that."

"To prom too. Your mother wore a white dress. She was a vision." Mr. Alderman smiles and pushes his glasses up on his nose.

"So. You're here. In Spalding. I thought you were in Ohio, wasn't it? When did you move back?" Mom's voice is a half-octave higher than normal.

"After my divorce." Mr. Alderman leans back against his desk.

"I'm sorry." Mom stiffens.

"Don't be. I'm not." He laughs and shrugs. Mom laughs too.

I cough loudly. "I'm gonna go."

Mom turns. "Right. I'll just text you when I'm done?"

"Great."

I hurry down the steps, across the courtyard and into the school through the back doors, then take off my mitts, shoving them under my armpit, and pull out my phone.

> Me: U will never believe this. My mom went to prom with Mr. Alderman. I just left them together in homeroom.

> Dace: No way!!

> Me: Think I'm in shock.

> Dace: At least u won't have to worry about acing English Lit this term.

It's 7:15, so I head back toward the main entrance, where Ben and I agreed to meet, but when I turn the corner to the main hallway he's coming toward me.

"Ms. Su grill you? I've never seen such strict rules on not having kids in a school." He grins.

"Yeah," I say, still thinking about Mom and Mr. Alderman.

I pull out the list of shots we still need—compiled mostly from the Facebook page—to distract myself.

The list is definitely getting shorter. "Janitor Jeb," I read out the next unchecked item on the list. We find him—a white-haired, Pooh-bellied old guy sitting on a step stool outside his closet, reading *His Mistress's Baby.* "You mind if we take your picture?" I ask, and he poses, delighted at the attention. I snap away while Ben holds out the reflector to soften the bad effects of shooting under fluorescent overhead lighting.

"Did you see how many of those books he had in his closet?" Ben says afterward.

"So awesome." I stop in front of a row of green lockers. "Locker 143," I read from the list.

"What's the story here?" Ben asks.

"Apparently it was the Hawker Locker for years—like a tuck shop but for old exams. The locker got passed down from one senior to the next. You'd made it if you got the lock to that locker. You got all the profits. One guy paid for a trip to Palm Beach for him and his four friends."

"Does the person say when the legacy died?"

"Nope. This guy graduated in '98."

"I would've kept that alive if I'd been here since freshman year," Ben says.

"Not surprising." I smirk at him: the jokes about his past bad behavior will never get old for me. The metal number plate takes up most of the frame, with just a hint of green around the edges. "Alright," I say a minute later, checking the list again. "Next up is a bird's-eye view of the football field from the top of the flagpole. Hmm, we're probably not allowed to do that."

"I'll do it quickly—no one will see," Ben says, and we head out the front doors. He reaches out and I hand him my camera. He slings it around his neck.

"You should chirp." Ben calls out while shimmying up the pole, his breath visible in the night air.

"Excuse me?"

"I'm getting a bird's-eye view and probably breaking some school rule and the chirping will be a sign that someone's coming. So I don't get busted."

"Why don't I just yell if I see someone?"

"The chirping is more covert. Just chirp."

I look around as a couple of people exit the front doors and head toward the parking lot. I chirp. Once.

Ben's holding the camera with one hand, his other deathgripping the pole as he takes the photo. He doesn't seem to hear my chirp.

I chirp louder. And again.

Ben slides down the pole. He hands the camera back to me and starts laughing. "I cannot believe you chirped. Those people are totally staring at you like you're a freak."

I smack him on the arm. "I hate you."

"Hatred makes the heart grow fonder."

"No one said that, ever."

● ● ●

"Just one shot left," I say nearly an hour later, sitting on the edge of the gym stage. "The inside of the gym storage room." I hop off the stage and cross the gym floor to the storage room. One of those plastic wedges holds the door slightly open.

Ben grabs the door handle and holds it open for me. The door clicks closed behind him. The air is a mix of rubber and mildew and the room is dark, the only light coming from the little window to the left of the door, which lets in a yellowish hue from the fluorescent lights in the gym.

"What's the deal with the Millers anyway?" he asks, referring to Mr. and Ms. Miller, the two PE teachers. "I've never seen such storage-room control freaks. Mr. Miller practically moonsaulted me when I tried to put my volleyball away."

"He practically *what-ted* you?"

"Moonsaulted. You know, WWE style."

I shake my head.

The middle of the room is packed with those metal cages filled with basketballs, volleyballs and utility balls. The walls are lined with skipping ropes hanging from hooks, nets and volleyball poles.

"You think this is Mr. and Mrs. Miller's secret love haven and that's why we're taking the picture?" Ben asks.

"Ew. What? They're brother and sister."

"No way. I thought they were married." Ben grabs a basketball and starts dribbling it.

"They look totally alike." I lean against the door.

"Ohhhh," Ben says, tossing the basketball in the air and catching it. "I thought they were like one of those old married couples that starts wearing orange fleece and Tilley hats and end up looking alike."

"They're more like the man-twins from the bus."

"So . . . if this isn't the spot for Miller Time, what's so great about this room?"

"Well, it is hook-up central, just not for the Millers. I figured you'd know."

Ben gives me the side eye. "I've only been here a semester. Besides it's not like I'm hooking up with every girl," he says. "Or, like, any girls." He shoots the basketball and it lands in the cage. "So what are you thinking for the shot?"

I look around. "If you're gonna do it in here, where's it happening?"

Ben winds his way through the cages. "Back here, on the mats. Check it out." He looks around, then grabs a rope mop from one of those yellow cleaning bins. It's dry and he lays it on the floor, the rope splayed at the top of the mat. Then he lies down and wraps his arms and legs around the mop in a tender embrace. "How's this look?" he asks, looking back at me, raising his eyebrows a few times.

"Like you're making out with a mop," I say, moving around to get an angle that might work. "Maybe I can mess with it in Photoshop, blur it out a bit and make the mop look like a human?"

"Matilda. Just don't do anything to her hair. She paid a fortune for her blonde highlights."

I snap away as Ben plays to the camera. "OK, wanna get out of here?" I shove my camera in my bag, as Ben gets up and heads for the door.

"Uh oh."

"What?"

"It's locked."

"But there's a wedge in the door."

"This one?" He bends down to pick up the chunk of brown plastic.

"Maybe this is why students aren't allowed in the school on parent-teacher night." I pull out my phone. "I'll text my mom. I'm sure someone in the office can open the door."

"Good thing I brought snacks." He pulls a mangled granola bar out of his coat pocket, and we settle down on the floor, leaning against the cages.

"How long has that been in there?"

"Well . . . I got it out of the vending machine at the bus terminal."

"At Port Authority?"

"No, in Spalding. On Saturday when I was—never mind. Want half?"

"This past Saturday? Why were you at the bus terminal on Saturday?"

"Nothing. Forget it." His face reddens.

"You're acting weird."

"It's because I'm hungry. I have to eat every two hours or I get cranky. Remember New York?"

"You did eat a lot."

He unwraps the bar and breaks it in two. He gives me the smaller half. "Sorry, but I need the fuel."

I take a bite. "Wow. Wow. This is terrible." For a split second I consider documenting the reverse Food Alert. Then remember there's no point. I push thoughts of Dylan away and pass the last bite to Ben.

"I guess that's what you get from a bus station vending machine."

"Yeah," I say slowly, trying to process what he didn't say.

"We've come a long way, huh Pip?" Ben says, wiping his hands on his jeans. "You can actually tolerate me. Maybe you do get a second chance to make a first impression."

I study his profile. "Actually, my first impression of you wasn't bad at all. Not that day you walked into the photocopy room." The sight of him leaning against the doorjamb pops into my head. I still remember exactly what he was wearing, the way his hair brushed across his forehead, the way his feet were crossed at the ankles.

"Really? What was it?"

"Oh, I don't know," I say quickly. "Just—maybe first impressions aren't everything."

"Maybe. I remember you that first day." He catches my eye and holds my gaze a split second longer than necessary.

"You do?" I say.

"Yeah." He leans closer to me, our bodies touching. I'm surprised, but I let him, feeling his warmth next to mine. Then his hands are on my face, pulling me in. I close my eyes as his lips meet mine. The kiss is soft, warm, and I wait for the butterflies, but they don't come. My stomach feels heavy and I remember our disastrous kissing session in Dace's room at her pool party. Him calling me "babe." Me not feeling 1% of the chemistry I have with Dylan. Had with Dylan. I open my eyes for a second, then close them again. It's no use. The kiss feels awkward, weird. I pull away just as the door opens.

"Well, well, well . . ." Mr. Miller says.

"We were taking photos," Ben says. "Except— not like that! For the alumni event. It's legit." Ben scrambles to his feet and pulls me up.

Mr. Miller doesn't seem to care what our excuse is, he just wants us out. I grab my coat off the ground and rush past Mr. Miller, Ben right behind me.

CHAPTER 21: THE DAY I'M SUPPOSED TO BE OVER HIM

When Dylan and I got together, I didn't really do that thing where you think ahead to special occasions—Will you be together on a birthday? Will you make it to Christmas?—because we were so *in the moment.* I don't know if I ever thought we wouldn't be together, or what, all I know is I just didn't think that far ahead. I wasn't worried. But since we broke up, there's been this voice I couldn't get rid of, even though I tried to ignore it, that would tell me, *Maybe you'll get back together by Valentine's Day. Give it time. Maybe by Valentine's Day . . .*

Even though today's the day I'm supposed to be over him. Even though we hadn't spoken, hadn't texted, hadn't seen each other since the breakup, I still couldn't help thinking: *Maybe. Maybe. Maybe.* But now, it's Valentine's Day, and I'm supposed to be lighthearted, carefree, able to move on. But I feel stuck. And my heart still feels broken.

The part of me that keeps thinking maybe he'll text today is screwed, because I left my phone in the storage room four days ago in my rush to get out of there, and the gym has been off-limits to everyone except teachers and the dance committee ever since with all the dance décor prep. No PE, no intra-murals, no phone rescue. No pleading has changed that: the dance committee had already covered over the storage room door with a huge poster that the senior art class painted. They refused to remove it because they claimed it would rip, and Mr. Miller said I'd have to wait until the dance was over to get my phone back, which was totally an unofficial punishment for being in there in the first place. It's been a pain for sure, but at least I've been getting to test Mom's "out of sight, out of mind" theory. I really, truly need to get over Dylan, especially since kissing Ben did nothing to distract me; instead it only triggered those feelings for Dylan that I'd been trying to quell.

"OK, OK," Mr. Alderman says, trying to quiet everyone down. But it's impossible. It's always like this on Valentine's Day—on account of the val-o-grams and the match-o-grams. For a dollar, you get to fill out a personality questionnaire with multiple-choice questions like, "The best thing you have going is: gut-splitting humor, super style or incredible intel-ligence" or "When you open your locker: it is tidy, there's a bit of clutter or it pours into the hall." The questionnaire is half the fun, and finding out who you're matched with is the other half. The only question it doesn't ask is about your gender and sexual preference; last year my tru lurve was Dace—which is way better than getting, like, Reggie. But sometimes you get matched with someone you actually like, and it ends up being just the push you need to talk to that person. That's what happened with Brendan and Abi last year, who both work on *Hall Pass*.

For another dollar, you can buy a val-o-gram, a chocolate heart taped to a note. You fill out the To and the From, and bam, your crush knows you like him or her.

Then, first thing on Valentine's Day, the student council drops off the match-os and val-os to every homeroom and they get distributed.

Mr. Alderman opens the bag and starts calling out the match-o-grams first. Dace always gets a ton of matches. You can kind of rig the match-o-gram if you think of the person you like when you fill it out. But while it worked out with Brendan and Abi, it never works out for any guys and Dace, on account of her ban on dating guys who go to our school. But she looks nervous as she opens her match-o-grams, because this year, she cares who she's matched with. Her regret over dumping Juan hasn't subsided one bit, and she shows me her card—his name isn't on it.

I get four matches—Jeffrey, from photo club; Ricardo, this new student who just moved here from Mexico City; Gemma and Ben. Ricardo sits in the next row over, so it's mildly awkward when we look at each other, but then I see he's got at least a dozen matches, so it's not like it's *that* awkward.

I show Ben's name to Dace. "What do you think it means?"

She gives me a look. "That algorithms suck?"

I laugh.

Gemma, Emma and Dace all give me val-o-grams. I sent one to them too, plus Lisa, since she's the editor at the paper, and Jeffrey, just because last year I was in homeroom with Jeffrey and he didn't get a single one, and I made a mental note to send him one this year, just because it would suck not to get any.

Dace gets 27 val-o-grams, including three from Hanif Jaffer, who reluctantly swapped lockers with me at the start of the year so I could be next to Dace. He's never recovered. But there's only one val-o-gram that has Dace blushing. Actually getting red in the face. She shows it to me. It's from Juan.

Then my name is called again. Alderman gives me an overly friendly smile, which he's been doing since he discovered my mom is his long-lost high school sweetheart, as he hands me the chocolate. I wait until I'm sitting to open the card.

To Wilbur. From BOB.

● ● ●

It was one thing to have a communication ban with Dylan for two weeks, but functioning without a cellphone for even a day, let alone four, is a lesson in how the world used to work. Or not. I leave Ben a note on his locker telling him to meet me in the gym at 6 to hang the mural. I'm late for third period after waiting at Dace's locker for her, to make sure we have a plan for the dance tonight. Then I set up the real plan for tonight: I hunt down Juan, spot him heading into the boys restroom after lunch, wait for him outside, then grab him and tell him that he clearly likes Dace and Dace likes him and that he has to show up at her house and take her to the dance. Instead of refusing, he looks like I've just made his day. And then asks me for reassurance that this is something she wants.

"Everyone keeps telling me not to bother with her—that she'll never date a guy in high school, let alone one that's younger than her. That she has a rule?"

"So *that's* why you've been so weird?" I say.

"Self-preservation. But I couldn't help myself with the val-o-gram."

I assure him he made the right move and that it was all a misunderstanding. He looks genuinely relieved. And for a split second, I feel like, *Wow, I am accomplishing stuff without a phone.* It's a small miracle.

●　●　●

Apparently half the dance committee wanted Winter Wonderland and the other half wanted Walk Down Memory Lane as the theme for the dance, so they compromised on "Winter Walk Down Memory Lane." The gym, as a result, is filled with miniature evergreens adorned with fake snow. White lights are strung from the ceiling, creating a snow/starry night effect, and the walls are covered in drapey white fabric. Ben's in the middle of the gym, holding a huge cardboard tube under his arm. A disco ball overhead speckles his body with swirling stars. It's the first time I've seen him since getting his val-o-gram and I'm not sure what to say. Things have been kind of awkward since the kiss—I kept thinking he'd bring it up, but he never did, and I certainly wasn't going to. The dance doesn't start for another hour, and the dance committee is bustling around. Ben's in a black suit and white shirt, open at the neck—his hair's slicked back and his eyes are kind of sparkling—but he doesn't look *hot*, just handsome. The feels, they just aren't there.

"You look great," he says, his tone friendly. "Shall we hang this sucker?" he says, pointing to a space on the wall the decorating committee left bare for us.

"Yeah," I say, distracted. He lays the roll on the ground and pulls the mural out.

I bend down, glad I opted for the dress I did—it's short, but stretchy, like one big teal tube top to mid-thigh, and then has this flowy, gauzy silvery overlay, so it's not at all scandalous, and I can actually move in it. I grab one end of the mural and hold it down as he unrolls it. We apply the adhesive strips, then move it over to the wall, fasten it and then stand back to see if it's straight.

"Wow. It looks better than I thought it would." I laid it out, so it's not like I haven't seen it before, but at this size, it's impressive.

"You did a kick-ass job."

"We did." I smile at him.

"Yeah, yeah. Hey," Ben says, looking around. "So, I don't really know how to bring this up. But we haven't talked about what happened the other day, in the . . . uh, storage room, and I know you have that whole equation thing, and I wanted to make sure I gave you time to get over Dylan. But I just didn't want you to think that it was just this random kiss, or whatever. I guess that's why I sent the val-o-gram."

"Oh," I say. "I didn't think it was random. And um, thanks?" I'm about to apologize for not sending one to him, but it would be the wrong message, and I'm psyching myself up to be totally honest with him about how I feel.

"OK. Good." He runs his hands through his hair, messing it a bit. "So, where are you on the equation timeline?"

"Today's supposed to be the last day. I'm supposed to be over him now."

"Wow, that's some timing."

"Yeah."

"So, are you?"

I bite my lip. "No."

Ben doesn't say anything for what seems like forever. Then he shoves his hands in his pockets. "OK."

"I'm sorry. You probably don't want to hear this, but I do want to be friends. If we can." I search his eyes and wait for him to say something.

He nods. "Friends. Sure. I'm a parakeet. You're a parakeet. Remember?" He grins.

I laugh. "Really?"

But a second later, his face changes, like he can't

pretend not to be disappointed. I've got gut-rot—that feeling you get after eating too much candy—but in this case, it's not too many Runts. He scratches the side of his face.

"The thing is, you've kind of become my best friend, Pippa. And I don't want to lose that. I feel like we *have* come a long way. And I really do like you, as a friend. But yeah, I guess there's no denying I have . . . some other feelings for you. So it's probably going to be a while before I'm ready to hear the details of how you and Dylan get back together."

"There it is!" a voice booms behind us. Principal Forsythe has his hands on his hips, taking in the mural. "This is impressive. *Impressive.*" He gesticulates at it, peers in for a moment, leans back again and then holds out his hand to shake mine, and then Ben's, and then he's skittering away.

Ben and I look at each other, bewildered by our preoccupied principal, and burst into laughter, the tension between us forgotten, at least for now.

● ● ●

I meet Mom by the staircase where the Glee club is singing love songs. She got her hair cut and colored after work today and her makeup done and she looks more dolled up than she has since before Dad got sick. She's wearing a really flattering green dress that matches her eyes.

"You look really pretty." I give her a hug.

"For an old lady?" She applies a light coral gloss to her lips and presses them together.

"You're far from old, Mom. Just wait till Hank sees you; he'll probably have a coronary."

She rolls her eyes but looks pleased. "Is there punch?"

"I think there very well may be," I say, and we link arms and make our way to the library, which has been transformed into a sort of bazaar—there's a candy bar, a poker table, the football team is raffling off old jerseys, the yearbook committee has set up a complicated game of Concentration using yearbook photos.

As we're standing in line to get drinks, a high-pitched voice says, "Holly?" and Mom turns.

"Kathryn!" The two embrace and then Mom gets out of line and starts chatting. I look around just as Dace walks into the library with Juan. "I can't believe you!" she squeals, rushing over to hug me.

"Do you know how hard it was to set you two up without a phone?"

"I love you. And I love your dress. You were right. This one is much more you. You look like a mermaid."

"Thanks," I say as the bartender hands me three glasses of sparkling juice. I pass two to Dace and Juan and then take the third for myself. "You look gorgeous." Dace is wearing a vintage dress that's creamy white lace up top with a pale pink tulle skirt that looks fantastic with her skin tone. Her hair's piled low on the side, a messy side-chignon.

"Is he here yet?"

"I haven't seen him, but I told him to find me in the library—easier since it's less crowded and brighter than the gym."

She squeezes my hands. "This is huge. I can't wait to meet him."

Juan tells Dace he's going to go say hi to his friends and she nods and then turns back to me.

"Did you talk to Ben?"

"I feel like a jerk. But he took it really well."

"You did the right thing. You can't force yourself to feel something that isn't there."

"I know. Did you . . . find anything out?"

"About Dylan? RFBR are on the schedule for 8:20 but Emma says the dance committee didn't ask for names of band members, so she has no idea if he'll show or not."

"I doubt he will. He was so against it."

"Yeah but would they really perform without their lead singer? Kind of a crap move."

I shrug.

"Maybe that's for the best. We can have a dance party fueled by too many cinnamon hearts, without you keeping one eye out for Dylan all night. Speaking of which, should we load up?" she asks and pulls me over to the candy bar. We grab cellophane bags and start scooping various pink, red and white candies into our little bags.

"Pippa." A voice says behind me. I turn to face David. He's clean-shaven and wearing a navy jacket over a dress shirt and skinny tie, with jeans and ankle boots. He takes off his cap and then leans forward to give me a hug. It's one of those loose, tentative hugs, like he's not even sure he should be hugging me.

"Hi," I say.

"Hi."

"This is Dace."

Dace sticks out her hand. David takes it. "The infamous Dace." He grins. "The top model."

"And you're the noted fashion photographer," Dace says without missing a beat. Juan comes back over, and David and I move away to talk.

"I'm really glad you came," I tell him.

"I'm glad you asked."

I nod, and look around.

"So, um, should we find my mom?"

He claps his hands together. "Let's do it."

"OK. Except, I actually don't know where she is. I would text her, except, you know, no phone. Oh, but you can."

"Let's be retro and just wander."

"Old school." I think of Dylan. Again. We're about to leave the library when I glance over to the far side, to the shelves of books. There's Mom. Between two stacks, her back's to us, but she's standing close to someone. I shift to get a better angle just as she takes a step back and I realize she wasn't just standing close to someone. She was kissing Mr. Alderman in the stacks.

I turn to face David, and he looks surprised, to say the least. I'm sure it wasn't the way he envisioned being reintroduced to Mom in person, but it's not as though he hasn't been party to a makeout session at a social event before.

"Maybe we should come back later?" David says.

"Yeah," I say, flustered.

We hustle out of the library.

"You OK?" he asks once we're out in the hall. "You seem a little shell-shocked."

"Yeah. That was my homeroom teacher. I mean, I knew my mom and him had history, but . . ." I feel like my eyes are as wide as saucers. "I didn't really process what might happen. I've never seen my mom kiss anyone other than my dad."

He grimaces. "A little weird?"

"A lot weird."

"Speaking of catching people locking lips . . ." He hesitates as we walk slowly down the hall. "Your mom told me that you saw me and Savida kissing at my party back in December. She gave me quite the talking-to. Totally deserved. I can only imagine how awful that was for you. I'm sorry—and believe me it will not happen again." He looks super embarrassed and I'm super embarrassed and thank god for Dace because she comes rushing up and saves me from having to say anything.

"Pip! It's 8:20," she says, raising her eyebrows meaningfully. I look at David but he shoos us.

"Go! Have fun. I'm going to wander."

And then Dace and I are off, rushing down the hall back to the gym. The doors are open and the familiar opening of "Where Are We Now?"—one of my favorite RFBR songs—begins. I squeeze through the crowd, trying to see the stage. There are five guys up there, but in the center, at the microphone, where Dylan should be, is someone else. Shorter. Darker skin. Longer hair. He starts singing the words I've heard Dylan sing so many times.

"*That* is definitely not Dylan," says Dace.

I feel a tap on my shoulder. I turn.

"Philadelphia Greene," Dylan says. My heart is pounding in my ears.

"Hi," I squeak out.

"Hi," he says. His eyes are warm.

Dace raises her eyebrows at me. "I'm going to, um, well, do something else, like not stand here right now," she says, not-so-subtly giving us some space.

"You're not up there," I say to Dylan. "But you're here."

"Surprising, I know, after I was all anti-reunion."

I offer a half-smile. "Is it weird to see—?"

"Yeah, kind of," he says, knowing that I mean him being here, back at Spalding. "I've started telling people why I'm on a break year."

"Wow." My heart starts beating more regularly, but my stomach is still doing flip-flops.

"So how are you?" Dylan asks. "Did you get . . ." He pauses, as though he wants to ask me something. I wait, because I'm not sure what he means. He clears his throat. "So how's Ben?"

"Good. I mean, I'm good. Well, I guess Ben's good too, but we're not . . . we worked on this project together," I say, pointing at the mural, "but that's it. I didn't. We're not—I . . ."

I want to tell him I'm still in love with him, but I don't have the courage.

"You look really pretty," he says. I can feel my face flush. He's wearing dark denim and a white button-down under a blue check blazer I've never seen before. But it's his eyes, his dimple, his lips I can't take my eyes off.

"Thanks. So do you."

"I've never been called pretty before," he jokes, and I feel my face get even hotter.

"So this." He nods at the mural. "This is a big deal."

"Thanks." I shift my weight from one foot to the other.

"Did you . . . ?" He pauses. "I was looking at it earlier. There's a lot on here I'd forgotten about." If he's seen the photo of himself, on the steps of the hospital, he doesn't mention it and I wonder if it's intentional, if that means something. That he doesn't want to bring us up? He points out the photos he really likes, and all I can think is how I've missed him, just being near him. His eyes, his laugh, his smile. I want to tell him that I don't want to be broken up with him. That I want to kiss him and have his arms around me, pulling me into him. I want to smell his cologne on my clothes after being with him. I want to feel his heart beating in his chest. The rule for how long it takes to get over someone may be right in some cases, but not this one. I'm nowhere close to being over Dylan. I don't *want* to get over Dylan. How can you get over someone you're still totally in love with? I have to tell him. In case there's even a small chance he feels the same way.

"Hey, I was wondering where you went."

Muse—looking like a boho princess in a long flowy floral skirt and wispy white top, her hair all wavy with a braid along the hairline—hands Dylan a glass of punch.

"Hi Pippa," she says, giving me an empty smile.

All of a sudden the lights are too bright, the music too loud. I blink, forcing myself to stay in the present.

"I was just talking to Pippa about this mural. She made it."

"Cool," Muse says, barely looking at it. She nods toward the stage. "These guys suck."

"This was actually my band," Dylan says, looking uncomfortable.

"Really?" Muse says, making a face. "Your music has evolved so much, DM."

My legs feel like they're going to give out. I clear my throat. "Anyway, I should go find Dace. See you later."

Dylan nods. "Yeah. OK. It was good to see you."

I mean to turn and walk away first, but Dylan says something to Muse and she nods, and then they turn toward the stage, winding their way through the crowd that sways to the music, until they disappear.

I slump against the wall, feeling defeated. Out of nowhere, Dace is there, leaning next to me. She rustles in her cellophane bag of candy, pulls one out, looks at it and gives it to me. It's one of those pastel-colored Valentine heart candies with a two-word message on it: *Love You.*

I pop it in my mouth. "Love you too."

Dace grabs my hand. "Let's dance."

● ● ●

David and I spend a while in front of the mural later, looking closely at it, studying it. He sees it as art, not just a fun alumni dance activity, like the photo booth or candy table. He talks about the lines in the football field, the light over darkness in a pic of an empty parking lot at the Spalding shopping mall.

When we're back out in the hallway, walking to my locker, he says, "The steps at the hospital—that one's your memory, right?" he says.

"How did you know?"

He tilts his head. "I can be a good listener occasionally. Nice leading lines with the steps."

That captured moment in time is more than a memory to me, and the lines in the photo are more than a technique. They're the tethers to my past—to the hospital, to Dad, to Dylan—which have led me to where I am right now. "I thought about using a different photo after Dylan and I broke up. Something that didn't have anything to do with him. But everything else felt like a lie."

"I like it," David says. "You're not rewriting history. Memories are important, even ones that are still painful."

"I'm ready for less pain." I fiddle with my clutch. David has the lowdown on the most recent Dylan-Muse situation, but I like that he's being real with me.

We stop in front of my locker and I spin the combination and open it, then take out the album.

"I never really thanked you for what a great mentor you were."

"Occasionally great," he says.

I laugh. "OK, so I feel kind of guilty taking credit for this, or saying it's a thank you for being my mentor or whatever. Because it's more than that. And it's also not really just my gift. It's something Dad wanted to do for you. I just . . . I found it on his computer. So I finished it. I guess, just—here." I shove it into his hands. He turns the book over, taking in both sides of the cover, then opens it slowly from the center—a trick so you don't crack the spine.

Then he goes through the first few pages.

I suddenly get self-conscious. Like, what if he thinks it's so weird, or something? "You don't have to look at it now."

"I didn't think he'd do it." Astonishment—thankful astonishment—fills his voice.

"What do you mean?"

"I asked your father for this. Well, not for this exactly. But for some photos of you. Of your life. This was when I knew . . . he wasn't doing well. I debated even asking, but I didn't want to bother your mom with it later, but there was this part of me—I had no idea you'd come to Tisch—that thought I'd never see you, let alone get to meet you and spend two weeks with you. So I sent your dad an email, asking him if he'd share some photos of you with me."

David continues flipping through the album, smiling and peering in closer at particular pages. He looks up at me. "Thank you, Pippa. For coming into my life. For coming back into my life. Just . . . thank you."

Two words. Right now, it's all I need.

CHAPTER 22: THE DAY AFTER

"Can we discuss Principal Forsythe's dance moves?" Dace says over breakfast the next morning. We're at home, sitting around the kitchen table—Mom, David, Dace and I. David slept at the Coach House Inn last night but got here around 10 this morning. Dace is here at Mom's suggestion, as a buffer so I wouldn't feel all, *Hey, here's me and my mom and Original/Replacement Dad, just having Saturday brunch together.* But we probably didn't need to worry—Mom and David have this really funny banter, nothing at all like her and Dad, and it's totally chill, like we do this all the time.

Mom's made her famous waffles, David's drinking coffee and Dace is popping up from her chair every few seconds to re-enact scenes from the dance. It's typical February weather outside—frigid—but the sun's streaming in the window and onto my skin. I look around and realize how nice this is. Mom's in a great mood (and I can't wait to tease her about Hank when we're alone), and David's heading back to New York tonight, but today, we're going to go on a photo tour of Spalding. He's got his old Nikon with him, and I've got Dad's, and we're going to shoot together while I show him around the town where I grew up.

"Oh my gosh, I almost forgot!" Dace shouts, hopping up from her seat, her mouth full of waffles. "After you left last night," says Dace a second later, "Juan and I broke into the storage room and got your phone back." She returns a minute later with it, holding it in the air like an Olympic torch. "It's dead." She plugs it into the charger on the wall by the coffee maker.

"Wow, thanks. But what about that huge poster? And how'd you get a key?"

Dace laughs and sits back down at the table, taking a swig of orange juice. "That poster caused a huge fight. When the dance committee saw that people were ripping it up they completely lost it, but hello, what were they going to do with it after the dance was over anyway? But yeah, so that was happening, and Juan somehow got the key, because he's a total badass—" Dace looks over at Mom, who's keeping her opinion to herself. "Uh . . . I don't really know how we got in. But Pip, your phone's back! Haven't you been dying without it?"

"It was kind of a relief, actually, to not have it," I say. Then I look toward Mom and David. "And to see how you guys possibly managed to function when you were our age."

My phone beeps a bunch of times as it comes to life and it's too much to resist. I stand up and grab it off the counter. Five days' worth of texts materialize on the screen. I swipe to see the messages. Mom, David, Ben . . . all before they knew I'd lost my phone, although Dace sent several last night. *Where are u? Pipster? Where arrrrrreeee youuuuu?* I look at her and she laughs. "Your non-replies are what reminded me," she says sheepishly, but I'm already looking at the other name on the unread texts: Dylan.

I can barely steady my hands enough to click on his name. Lines and lines of text fill the screen.

Dylan: Favorite memory of Spalding: you.

And then, next, there's a photo, a selfie of the two of us from our mini-Christmas together, when we exchanged gifts at his place, in his room. And then:

Pretty sure this is too late for your mural, and you probably wouldn't have wanted a pic of us on it anyway. And actually it doesn't even have anything to do with Spalding, but when I think of the school, I think of you. And I wanted you to have this photo. I'm not sure if you remember, but I took this right after we'd opened our Xmas gifts. I know we can't get back to how happy we were then, and I know that's not what you want, but I didn't want us to end things as strangers. Maybe we can't be friends. But at least know I think of you like that. And I always will.

I stare at his words, scrolling back up and reading them again, until Dace interrupts.

"What?" Dace says. "What are you reading? What does it say?"

I hand her the phone. Mom and David have taken their coffees into the living room.

"Wow," Dace says a minute later. "When did he send this?" She scrolls up the screen. "Two days ago." She looks at me. "Before you two saw each other. Do you think . . . ?"

My eyes have filled with tears. I take a few deep breaths.

"What does this even mean?"

"Maybe just what he said. He wants to make amends. To leave things on a good note? So when you think of him and what you guys had, you remember the good stuff, and not the way it ended. Isn't that better than hating him forever?"

I think about that quote "Good things don't end." Things were good with Dylan. And then they weren't. I think about Mom and David, how things ended so badly with them, but how that pushed Dad to tell Mom how he felt about her. And that turned into Dad being the only father I ever knew. If things hadn't ended badly between Mom and David, how differently would my life have turned out? I don't have the answer, but I know I don't need it. Mom and David have made amends now, and everything's out in the open.

I look in the living room and see Mom sitting next to David, the two of them laughing, clearly getting along, and I think maybe Dylan has it right, as mixed up as I feel about him. Maybe remembering the good times will get us through to the next stage in our relationship or friendship or whatever our not-strangers phase will be.

Dace hands my phone back to me. "Are you OK?" she asks, giving me a bear hug.

I squeeze her tight. "No, not yet. But I'll get there."

ACKNOWLEDGMENTS

I'm so lucky to have the wonderful ECW Press as my publisher. Thanks in particular to: Jack David, David Caron, Laura Pastore, Troy Cunningham, Rachel Ironstone, Lynn Gammie, Erin Creasey, Jenna Illies and Susannah Ames, who have all put so much energy into making this third book in the Pippa series as special as the first; my all-star editor, Crissy Calhoun, who feels like Pippa's real-life BFF and always gives me such valuable guidance, editing and advice; and Jen Knoch, whose comments in the margins never fail to make me laugh; first readers Marissa Stapley for the working pool days that remind me how fun it is to be a writer; Janis Leblanc, who was at the ready so often to help me answer What Would Pippa Do; Sarah Hartley, for her thoughtful notes; and my parents Michel and Susan Guertin and parents-in-law Myron and Nancy

Shulgan for the hours and hours (okaaaay, days) of free babysitting so I can write, and all of my family and friends for simply being there. Most of all, to Chris, for all the roles he plays in my life: editor, supporter, love of my life, and number-one crush.

CHANTEL GUERTIN is the bestselling author of four novels—*Stuck in Downward Dog, Love Struck, The Rule of Thirds* and *Depth of Field*—and a beauty expert on *The Marilyn Denis Show*. When she's not working on a new book, she likes writing in her diary, sending mis-autocorrected texts to her best friends and making to-do lists. She lives in Toronto, Ontario.

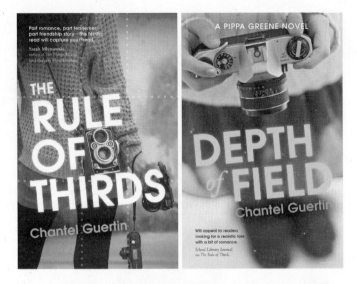

ALSO IN THE SERIES

At ECW Press, we want you to enjoy *Leading Lines* in whatever format you like, whenever you like. Leave your print book at home and take the eBook to go! Purchase the print edition and receive the eBook free. Just send an email to ebook@ecwpress.com and include:

- the book title
- the name of the store where you purchased it
- your receipt number
- your preference of file type: PDF or ePub?

A real person will respond to your email with your eBook attached. And thanks for supporting an independently owned Canadian publisher with your purchase!